JAC...

Jack Higgins lived .... till the age of twelve. Leaving school at fifteen, he spent three years with the Royal Horse Guards, serving on the East German border during the Cold War. His subsequent employment included occupations as diverse as circus roustabout, truck driver, clerk and, after taking an honours degree in sociology and social psychology, teacher and university lecturer.

The Eagle Has Landed turned him into an international bestselling author, and his novels have since sold over 250 million copies and have been translated into fifty-five languages. Many of them have also been made into successful films. His recent bestselling novels include, *Bad Company*, *A Fine Night for Dying*, *Dark Justice*, *The Killing Ground*, *Rough Justice*, *A Darker Place* and *The Wolf at the Door*.

In 1995 Jack Higgins was awarded an honorary doctorate by Leeds Metropolitan University. He is a fellow of the Royal Society of Arts and an expert scuba diver and marksman. He lives on Jersey.

ALSO BY JACK HIGGINS

JACK HIGGINS

THE LAST PLACE GOD MADE

HARPER

Harper
An imprint of HarperCollins*Publishers*
77–85 Fulham Palace Road,
Hammersmith, London w6 8jb

www.harpercollins.co.uk

This paperback edition 2010
This production 2013

First published in Great Britain by
William Collins Sons & Co 1971
Published in Signet 1997

Copyright © Jack Higgins 1971

Jack Higgins asserts the moral right to
be identified as the author of this work

A catalogue record for this book is
available from the British Library

ISBN: 978-0-00-793361-7

Typeset in Sabon by Palimpsest Book Production Limited,
Grangemouth, Stirlingshire

Printed and bound in Great Britain by
Clays Ltd, St Ives plc

MIX
Paper from
responsible sources
FSC™ C007454

FSC™ is a non-profit international organisation established to promote
the responsible management of the world's forests. Products carrying the
FSC label are independently certified to assure consumers that they come
from forests that are managed to meet the social, economic and
ecological needs of present and future generations,
and other controlled sources.

Find out more about HarperCollins and the environment at
www.harpercollins.co.uk/green

PUBLISHER'S NOTE

The Last Place God Made was first published in the UK by William Collins Sons & Co. Ltd in 1971 and later by Signet in 1997. This amazing novel has been out of print for some years, and in 2010, it seemed to the author and his publishers that it was a pity to leave such a good story languishing on his shelves. So we are delighted to be able to bring back *The Last Place God Made* for the pleasure of the vast majority of us who never had a chance to read the earlier editions.

FOREWORD

Small planes feature in many of my books. I can't fly them myself, but I travel in them a great deal. My wife, Denise, is a qualified pilot, and she provides any expertise I need about flying. *The Last Place God Made* concerns a First World War Bristol fighter being used in the Amazon in 1939 to fly mail.

When I was a young man in Leeds, a close friend's father used to tell us of his experiences flying a Bristol in Russia in 1919. He was awarded the DFC while serving with an RAF squadron in Archangel, helping the white Russians against what were then known as the Reds. His exciting stories sparked my interest in flying.

CONTENTS

And this one is for my sister-in-law,
Babs Hewitt, who is absolutely certain
it's about time . . .

1

Ceiling Zero

When the port wing began to flap I knew I was in trouble, not that I hadn't been for some little time. Oil pressure mainly plus a disturbing miss in the beat of the old Pratt and Whitney Wasp engine that put me uncomfortably in mind of the rattle in a dying man's throat.

The Vega had been good enough in its day. Typical of that sudden rush of small high-winged, single-engined airliners that appeared in the mid-1920s. Built to carry mail and half a dozen passengers at a hundred or so miles an hour.

The one I was trying to keep in the air at that precise moment in time had been built in 1927 which made it eleven years old. Eleven years of flying mail in every kind of weather. Of inadequate servicing. Of over use.

She'd been put together again after no fewer than three crash landings and that was only what was officially entered in the log. God alone knows what had been missed out.

Kansas, Mexico, Panama, Peru, sinking a little lower with each move, finding it that much more difficult to turn in her best performance, like a good horse being worked to death. Now, she was breaking up around me in the air and there wasn't much I could do about it.

From Iquitos in Peru, the Amazon river twists like a brown snake through two thousand miles of some of the worst jungle in the world, its final destination Belem on the Atlantic coast of Brazil with Manaus at the junction with the Rio Negro, the halfway point and my present destination.

For most of the way, I'd followed the river which at least made for easy navigation, alone with three sacks of mail and a couple of crates of some kind of mining machinery. Six long, hard hours to Tefé and I managed to raise three police posts on the way on my radio although things were quiet as the grave at Tefé itself.

From there, the river drifted away in a great, wide loop and to have followed it would have made the run to Manaus another four hundred miles and the Vega just didn't have that kind of fuel in reserve.

From Tefé, then, I struck out due east across virgin jungle, aiming for the Rio Negro a hundred and fifty miles farther on where a turn downstream would bring me to Manaus.

It had been a crazy venture from the first, a flight that to my knowledge no one had accomplished at that time and yet at twenty-three, with the sap rising, a man tends to think himself capable of most things and Belem was, after all, two thousand miles closer to England than the point from which I'd started and a passage home at the end of it.

Yet I see now, looking back on it all after so many years, how much in the whole affair was the product of chance, that element quite beyond calculation in a man's affairs.

To start with, my bold plunge across such a wide stretch of virgin jungle was not quite as insane as it might appear. True, any attempt at dead reckoning was ruled out by the simple fact that my drift indicator was not working and the magnetic compass was wholly unreliable, but the Rio Negro did lie a hundred and fifty miles due east of Tefé, that was fact, and I had the sun to guide me in a sky so crystal clear that the horizon seemed to stretch to infinity.

Falling oil pressure was the first of my woes although I didn't worry too much about that to start with for the Oil Pressure Gauge, like most of the instruments, frequently didn't work at all and was at best, less than reliable.

And then, unbelievably, the horizon broke into a series of jagged peaks almost before my eyes, something else about which I couldn't really complain for on the map, that particular section was merely a blank space.

Not that they were the Andes exactly, but

high enough, considering the Vega's general condition, although the altimeter packed in at four thousand feet, so everything after that was guesswork.

The sensible way of doing things would have been to stay far enough from them to be out of harm's way and then to gain the correct height to cross the range by flying round and round in upward spirals for as long as may be. But I didn't have time enough for that, by which I mean fuel and simply eased back the stick and went in on the run.

I don't suppose there was more than four or five hundred feet in it as I started across the first great shoulder that lifted in a hog's back out of the dark green of the rain forest. Beyond, I faced a scattering of jagged peaks and not too much time for decisions.

I took a chance, aimed for the gap between the two largest and flew on over a landscape so barren that it might have been the moon. I dropped sickeningly in an air pocket, the Vega protesting with every fibre of its being and I eased back the stick again as the ground rose to meet me.

For a while it began to look as if I'd made a bad mistake for the pass through which I was flying narrowed considerably so that at one point, there seemed every chance of the wing-tips brushing the rock face. And then, quite suddenly, I lifted over a great, fissured ridge with no more than a hundred feet to spare and found myself flying across an enormous valley, mist rising to engulf me like steam from a boiling pot.

Suddenly, it was a lot colder and rain drifted across the windshield in a fine spray and then the horizon of things crackled with electricity as rain swept in from the east in a great cloud to engulf me.

Violent tropical storms of that type were one of the daily hazards of flying in the area. Frequent and usually short-lived, they could wreak an incredible amount of damage and the particular danger was the lightning associated with them. It was usually best to climb over them, but the Vega was already as high as she was going to go considering the state she was in so I really had no other choice than to hang on and hope for the best.

I didn't think of dying, I was too involved in keeping the plane in the air to have time for anything else. The Vega was made of wood. Cantilevered wings and streamlined wooden skin fuselage, manufactured in two halves and glued together like a child's toy and now, the toy was tearing itself to pieces.

Outside, it was almost completely dark and water cascaded in through every strained seam in the fuselage as we rocked in the turbulence. Rain streamed from the wings, lightning flickering at their tips and pieces of fuselage started to flake away.

I felt a kind of exultation more than anything else at the sheer involvement of trying to control that dying plane and actually laughed out loud at one point when a section of the roof went and water cascaded in over my head.

I came out into bright sunlight of the late afternoon and saw the river on the horizon immediately. It had to be the Negro and I pushed the Vega towards it, ignoring the stench of burning oil, the rattling of the wings.

Pieces were breaking away from the fuselage

constantly now and the Vega was losing height steadily. God alone knows what was keeping the engine going. It was really quite extraordinary. Any minute now, and the damn thing might pack up altogether and a crash landing in that impenetrable rain forest below was not something I could reasonably hope to survive.

A voice crackled in my earphone. 'Heh, Vega, your wings are flapping so much I thought you were a bird. What's keeping you up?'

He came up from nowhere and levelled out off my port wing, a Hayley monoplane in scarlet and silver trim, no more than four or five years old from the look of it. The voice was American and with a distinctive harshness to it that gave it its own flavour in spite of the static that was trying to drown it.

'Who are you?'

'Neil Mallory,' I said. 'Iquitos for Belem by way of Manaus.'

'Jesus.' He laughed harshly. 'I thought it was Lindberg they called the flying fool.

Manaus is just on a hundred miles downriver from here. Can you stay afloat that long?'

Another hour at least. I checked the fuel gauge and air-speed indicator and faced the inevitable. 'Not a chance. Speed's falling all the time and my tank's nearly dry.'

'No use jumping for it in this kind of country,' he said. 'You'd never be seen again. Can you hold her together for another ten minutes?'

'I can try.'

'There's a patch of *campo* ten or fifteen miles downstream. Give you a chance to land that thing if you're good enough.'

I didn't reply because the fuselage actually started to tear away in a great strip from the port wing and the wing, as if in pain, moved up and down more frantically than ever.

I was about a thousand feet up as we reached the Negro and turned downstream, drifting gradually and inevitably towards the ground like a falling leaf. There was sweat on my face in spite of the wind rushing in through the holes in the fuselage and my hands were cramped tight on the stick for it was taking all my strength to hold her.

'Easy, kid, easy.' That strange, harsh voice crackled through the static. 'Not long now. A mile downstream on your left. I'd tell you to start losing height only you're falling like a stone as it is.'

'I love you too,' I said and clamped my teeth hard together and held on as the Vega lurched violently to starboard.

The *campo* blossomed in the jungle a quarter of a mile in front of me, a couple of hundred yards of grassland beside the river. The wind seemed to be in the right direction although in the state the Vega was in, there wasn't much I could have done about it if it hadn't been. I hardly needed to throttle back to reduce airspeed for my approach – the engine had almost stopped anyway – but I got the tail trimmer adjusted and dropped the flaps as I floated in across the tree-tops.

It took all my sterngth to hold her, stamping on the rudder to pull her back in line as she veered to starboard. It almost worked. I plunged down, with a final burst of power to level out for my landing and the engine chose that precise moment to die on me.

It was like running slap into an invisible wall. The Vega seemed to hang there in the air a hundred feet above the ground for a moment, then swooped.

I left the undercarriage in the branches of the trees at the west end of the *campo*. In fact I think, in the final analysis, that was what saved me for the braking effect on the plane as she barged through the top of the trees was considerable. She simply flopped down on her belly on the *campo* and ploughed forward through the six-foot-high grass, leaving both wings behind her on the way and came to a dead halt perhaps twenty yards from the bank of the river.

I unstrapped my seat belt, kicked open the door, threw out the mail bags and followed them through, just in case. But there was no need and the fact that she hadn't gone up like a torch on impact wasn't luck. It was simply that there wasn't anything left in the tanks to burn.

I sat down very carefully on one of the mail sacks. My hands were trembling slightly – not much, but enough – and my heart was pounding like a trip-hammer. The Hayley swooped low overhead. I waved without looking up, then unzipped my flying jacket and found a tin of Balkan Sobranie cigarettes, last of a carton I'd bought on the black market in Lima the previous month. I don't think anything in life to that moment had ever tasted as good.

After a while, I stood up and turned in time to see the Hayley bank and drop in over the trees on the far side of the *campo*. He made it look easy and it was far from that, for the wreckage of the Vega and the position where its wings had come to rest in its wake left him very little margin for error. There couldn't have been more than a dozen yards between the tip of his port wing and the edge of the trees.

I sat down on one of the mail sacks again, mainly because my legs suddenly felt very weak and lit another Sobranie. I could hear him ploughing towards me through the long grass, and once he called my name. God knows why I didn't answer. Some kind of shock. I suppose. I simply sat there, the cigarette slack between my lips and stared beyond the wreck of the Vega to the river, taking in every sight and sound in minute detail as if to prove I was alive.

'By God, you can fly, boy. I'll say that for you.'

He emerged from the grass and stood looking at me, hands on hips in what I was to learn was an inimitable gesture. He was physically very big indeed and wore a leather top-coat, breeches, knee-length boots, a leather helmet, goggles pushed up high on the forehead and there was a .45 Colt automatic in a holster on his right thigh.

I put out my hand and when I spoke, the voice seemed to belong to someone else. 'Mallory – Neil Mallory.'

'You already told me that – remember?' He grinned. 'My name's Hannah – Sam Hannah. Anything worth salvaging in there besides the mail?'

As I discovered later, he was forty-five years

of age at that time, but he could have been older or younger if judged on appearance alone for he had one of those curiously ageless faces, tanned to almost the same colour as his leather coat.

He had the rather hard, self-possessed, competent look of a man who had been places and done things, survived against odds on occasions and yet, even from the first, there seemed a flaw in him. He made too perfect a picture standing there in his flying kit, gun on hip, like some R.F.C. pilot waiting to take off on a dawn patrol across the trenches, yet more like a man playing the part than the actuality. And the eyes were wrong – a sort of pale, washed blue that never gave anything away.

I told him about the mining machinery and he climbed inside the Vega to look for himself. He reappeared after a while holding a canvas grip.

'This yours?' I nodded and he threw it down. 'Those crates are out of the question. Too heavy for the Hayley anyway. Anything else you want?'

14

I shook my head and then remembered. 'Oh yes, there's a revolver in the map compartment.'

He found it with no difficulty and pushed it across, together with a box of cartridges, a Webley .38 which I shoved away in one of the pockets of my flying jacket.

'Then if you're ready, we'll get out of here.' He picked up the three mail sacks with no visible effort. 'The Indians in these parts are Jicaros. There were around five thousand of them till last year when some doctor acting for one of the land companies infected them with smallpox instead of vaccinating them against it. The survivors have developed the unfortunate habit of skinning alive any white man they can lay hands on.'

But such tales had long lost the power to move me for they were commonplace along the Amazon at a time when most settlers or prospectors regarded the Indians as something other than human. Vermin to be ruthlessly stamped out and any means were looked upon as fair.

I stumbled along behind Hannah who kept up a running conversation, cursing freely as great clouds of grasshoppers and insects of various kinds rose in clouds as we disturbed them.

'What a bloody country. The last place God made. As far as I'm concerned, the Jicaros can have it and welcome.'

'Then why stay?' I asked him.

We had reached the Haley by then and he heaved the mail bags inside and turned, a curious glitter in his eyes. 'Not from choice, boy, I can tell you that.'

He gave me a push up into the cabin. It wasn't as large as the Vega. Seats for four passengers and a freight compartment behind, but everything was in apple-pie order and not just because she wasn't all that old. This was a plane that enjoyed regular, loving care. Something I found faintly surprising because it didn't seem to fit with Hannah.

I strapped myself in beside him and he closed the door. 'A hundred and eighty this baby does at full stretch. You'll be wallowing in a hot bath before you know it.' He grinned.

'All right, tepid, if I know my Manaus plumbing.'

Suddenly I was very tired. It was marvellous just to sit there, strapped comfortably into my seat and let someone else do the work and as I've said, he was good. Really good. There wasn't going to be more than a few feet in it as far as those trees were concerned at the far end of the *campo* and yet I hadn't a qualm as he turned the Hayley into the wind and opened the throttle.

He kept her going straight into that green wall, refusing to sacrifice power for height, waiting until the last possible moment, pulling the stick back into his stomach and lifting us up over the tops of the trees with ten feet to spare.

He laughed out loud and slapped the bulkhead with one hand. 'You know what's the most important thing in life, Mallory? Luck – and I've got a bucket full of the stuff. I'm going to live to be a hundred and one.'

'Good luck to you,' I said.

Strange, but he was like a man with drink taken. Not drunk, but unable to stop talking.

For the life of me, I can't remember what he said, for gradually my eyes closed and his voice dwindled until it was one with the engine itself and then, that too faded and there was only the quiet darkness.

2

Maria of the Angels

I had hoped to be on my way in a matter of hours, certainly no later than the following day for in spite of the fact that Manaus was passing through hard times, there was usually a boat of some description or another leaving for the coast most days.

Things started to go wrong from the beginning. To start with, there was the police in the person of the *comandante* himself who insisted on giving me a personal examination regarding the crash, noting my every word in his own hand which took up a remarkable amount of time.

After signing my statement I had to wait outside his office while he got Hannah's version of the affair. They seemed to be old and close friends from the laughter echoing faintly through the closed door and when they finally emerged, Hannah had an arm round the *comandante's* shoulder.

'Ah, Senhor Mallory.' The *comandante* nodded graciously. 'I have spoken to Captain Hannah on this matter and am happy to say that he confirms your story in every detail. You are free to go.'

Which was nice of him. He went back into his office and Hannah said, 'That's all right, then.' He frowned as if concerned and put a hand on my shoulder. 'I've got things to do, but you look like the dead walking. Grab a cab downstairs and get the driver to take you to the Palace Hotel. Ask for Senhor Juca. Tell him I sent you. Five or six hours' sleep and you'll be fine. I'll catch up with you this evening. We'll have something to eat. Hit the high spots together.'

'In Manaus?' I said.

'They still have their fair share of sin if you know where to look.' He grinned crookedly. 'I'll see you later.'

He returned to the *comandante's* office, opening the door without knocking and I went downstairs and out through the cracked marble pillars at the entrance.

I didn't go to the hotel straight away. Instead, I took one of the horse-drawn cabs that waited at the bottom of the steps and gave the driver the address of the local agent of the mining company for whom I'd contracted to deliver the Vega to Belem.

In its day during the great rubber boom at the end of the nineteenth century, Manaus had been the original hell-hole, millionaires walking the streets ten-a-penny, baroque palaces, an opera house to rival Paris itself. No sin too great, no wickedness too evil. Sodom and Gomorrah rolled into one and set down on the banks of the Negro, a thousand miles up the Amazon.

I had never cared much for the place. There was a suggestion of corruption, a kind of general decay. A feeling that the jungle was gradually creeping back in and that none of us had any right to be there.

I felt restless and ill-at-ease, reaction to stress,

I suppose, and wanted nothing so much as to be on my way, looking back on this place over the sternrail of a riverboat for the last time.

I found the agent in the office of a substantial warehouse on the waterfront. He was tall, cadaverous, with the haunted eyes of a man who knows he has not got long to live and he coughed repeatedly into a large, soiled handkerchief which was already stained with blood.

He gave thanks to Our Lady for my deliverance to the extent of crossing himself and in the same breath pointed out that under the terms of my contract, I only got paid on safe delivery of the Vega to Belem. Which was exactly what I had expected and I left him in a state of near collapse across his desk doing his level best to bring up what was left of his lungs and went outside.

My cab still waited for me, the driver dozing in the heat of the day, his straw sombrero tilted over his eyes. I walked across to the edge of the wharf to see what was going on in the basin which wasn't much, but there was a stern-wheeler up at the next wharf loading green bananas.

I found the captain in a canvas chair under an awning on the bridge and he surfaced for as long as it took to tell me he was leaving at nine the following morning for Belem and that the trip would take six days. If I didn't fancy a hammock on deck with his more impoverished customers, I could have the spare bunk in the mate's cabin with all found for a hundred *cruzeiros*. I assured him I would be there on time and he closed his eyes with complete indifference and returned to more important matters.

I had just over a thousand *cruzeiros* in my wallet, around a hundred and fifty pounds sterling at that time which meant that even allowing for the trip down-river and incidental expenses, I would have ample in hand to buy myself a passage to England from Belem on some cargo boat or other.

I was going home. After two and a half years of the worst that South America could offer, I was on my way and it felt marvellous. Definitely one of life's great moments and all tiredness left me as I turned and hurried back to the cab.

* * *

I had expected the worst of the hotel but the Palace was a pleasant surprise. Certainly it had seen better days, but it had a kind of baroque dignity to it, a faded charm that was very appealing, and Hannah's name had a magic effect on the Senhor Juca he had mentioned, an old, white-haired man in an alpaca jacket who sat behind the desk reading a newspaper.

He took me upstairs personally and ushered me into a room with its own little ironwork terrace overlooking the river. The whole place was a superb example of late Victoriana, caught for all time like a fly in amber from the brass bed to the heavy, mahogany furniture.

An Indian woman in a black bombazine dress appeared with clean sheets and the old man showed me, with some pride, the bathroom next door of which I could have sole use, although regrettably it would be necessary to ring for hot water. I thanked him for his courtesy, but he waved his hands deprecatingly and assured me, with some eloquence, that nothing was too much trouble for a friend of Captain Hannah's.

24

I thought about that as I undressed. Whatever else you could say about him, Hannah obviously enjoyed considerable standing in Manaus which was interesting, considering he was a foreigner.

I needed that bath badly, but suddenly, sitting there on the edge of the bed after getting my boots off, I was overwhelmed with tiredness. I climbed between the sheets and was almost instantly asleep.

I surfaced to the mosquito net billowing above me like a pale, white flower in the breeze from the open window and beyond, a face floated disembodied in the diffused yellow glow of an oil lamp.

Old Juca blinked sad, moist eyes. 'Captain Hannah was here earlier, senhor. He asked me to wake you at nine o'clock.'

It took its own time in getting through to me. 'Nine o'clock?'

'He asks you to meet him, senhor, at *The Little Boat*. He wishes you to dine with him. I have a cab waiting to take you there, senhor. Everything is arranged.'

'That's nice of him,' I said, but any iron in my voice was obviously lost on him.

'Your bath is waiting, senhor. Hot water is provided.'

He put the lamp down carefully on the table, the door closed with a gentle sigh behind him, the mosquito net fluttered in the eddy like some great moth, then settled again.

Hannah certainly took a lot for granted. I got up, feeling vaguely irritated at the way things were being managed for me and padded across to the open window. Quite suddenly, my whole mood changed for it was pleasantly cool after the heat of the day, the breeze perfumed with flowers. Lights glowed down there on the river and music echoed faintly, the freedom from the sound of it, pulsating through the night, filling me with a vague, irrational excitement.

When I turned back to the room I made another discovery. My canvas grip had been unpacked and my old linen suit had been washed and pressed and hung neatly from the back of a chair waiting for me. There was really nothing I could do, the pressures were too great, so I gave in gracefully, found a towel and went along the corridor to have my bath.

Although the main rainy season was over, rainfall always tends to be heavy in the upper Amazon basin area and sudden, violent downpours are common, especially at night.

I left the hotel to just such a rush of rain and hurried down the steps to the cab which was waiting for me, escorted by Juca who insisted on holding an ancient black umbrella over my head. The driver had raised the leather hood which kept out most of the rain if not all and drove away at once.

The streets were deserted, washed clean of people by the rain and from the moment we left the hotel until we reached our destination, I don't think we saw more than half a dozen people, particularly when we moved through the back streets towards the river.

We emerged on the waterfront at a place where there were a considerable number of houseboats of various kinds for a great many people actually lived on the river this way.

We finally came to a halt at the end of a long pier.

'This way, senhor.'

The cabby insisted on placing his old oilskin coat about my shoulders and escorted me to the end of the pier where a lantern hung from a pole above a rack festooned with fishing nets.

An old riverboat was moored out there in the darkness, lights gleaming, laughter and music drifting across the water. He leaned down and lifted a large, wooden trapdoor and the light from the lamp flooded in to reveal a flight of wooden steps. He went down and I followed without hesitation. I had, after all, no reason to expect foul play and in any event, the Webley .38 which I'd had the forethought to slip into my right-hand coat pocket was as good an insurance as any.

A kind of boardwalk stretched out through the darkness towards the riverboat, constructed over a series of canoes and it dipped alarmingly as we moved across.

When we reached the other end the cabby smiled and slapped the hull with the flat of his palm. '*The Little Boat*, senhor. Good appetite in all things but in food and women most of all.'

It was a Brazilian saying and well intended. I reached for my wallet and he raised a hand. 'It is not necessary, senhor. The good captain has seen to it all.'

Hannah again. I watched him negotiate the swaying catwalk successfully as far as the pier then turned and went up some iron steps which took me to the deck. A giant of a man moved from the shadows beside a lighted doorway, a Negro with a ring in one ear and a heavy, curly beard.

'Senhor?' he said.

'I'm looking for Captain Hannah,' I told him. 'He's expecting me.'

The teeth gleamed in the darkness. *Another friend of Hannah's.* This was really beginning to get monotonous. He didn't say anything, simply opened the door for me and I passed inside.

I suppose it must have been the main saloon in the old days. Now it was crowded with tables, people crammed together like sardines. There was a permanent curtain of smoke that, allied to the subdued lighting, made visibility a problem, but I managed to detect a bar in one corner on the other side of the small, packed dance floor. A five-piece rumba band was banging out a *carioca* and most of the crowd seemed to be singing along with it.

I saw Hannah in the thick of it on the floor dancing about as close as it was possible to get to a really beautiful girl by any standards. She was of mixed blood, Negro-European variety was my guess and wore a dress of scarlet satin that fitted her like a second skin and made her look like the devil's own.

He swung her round, saw me and let out a great cry. 'Heh, Mallory, you made it.'

He pushed the girl away as if she didn't exist and ploughed through the crowd towards me. Nobody got annoyed even when he put a drink or two over. Mostly they just smiled and one or two of the men slapped him on the back and called good-naturedly.

He'd been drinking, that much was obvious and greeted me like a long lost brother. 'What kept you? Christ, but I'm starving. Come on, I've got a table laid on out on the terrace where we can hear ourselves think.'

He took me by the elbow and guided me through the crowd to a long, sliding shutter on the far side. As he started to pull it back, the girl in the red satin dress arrived and flung her arms around his neck.

He grabbed her wrists and she gave a short cry of pain, that strength of his again, I suppose. He no longer looked anything like as genial and somehow, his bad Portuguese made it sound worse.

'Later, angel – later, I'll screw you just as much as you damn well want only now, I want a little time with my friend. Okay?'

When he released her she backed away, looked scared if anything, turned and melted into the crowd. I suppose it was about then I noticed that the women vastly outnumbered the men and commented on the fact.

'What is this, a whorehouse?'

'Only the best in town.'

He pulled back the shutter and led the way out to a private section of the deck with a canvas awning from which the rain dripped steadily. A table, laid for two, stood by the rail under a pressure lamp.

He shouted in Portuguese, 'Heh, Pedro, let's have some action here.' Then he motioned me to one of the seats and produced a bottle of wine from a bucket of water under the table. 'You like this stuff – Pouilly Fuisse? They get it for me special. I used to drink it by the bucketful in the old days in France.'

I tried some. It was ice-cold, sharp and fresh and instantly exhilarating. 'You were on the Western Front?'

'I sure was. Three years of it. Not many lasted that long, I can tell you.'

Which at least explained the Captain bit. I said, 'But America didn't come into the war till nineteen-seventeen.'

'Oh, that.' He leaned back out of the way as a waiter in a white shirt and cummerbund appeared with a tray to serve us. 'I flew for the French with the Lafayette Escadrille. Nieuport Scouts then Spads.' He leaned forward to refill my glass. 'How old are you, Mallory?'

'Twenty-three.'

He laughed. 'I'd twenty-six kills to my credit when I was your age. Been shot down four times, once by von Richthofen himself.'

Strange, but at that stage of things I never doubted him for a second. Stated baldly, what he had said could easily sound like boasting and yet it was his manner which said most and he was casual in the extreme as if these things were really of no account.

We had fish soup, followed by a kind of casserole of chicken stewed in its own blood, which tasted a lot better than it sounds. This was backed up by eggs and olives fried, as usual, in olive oil. And there was a mountain of rice and tomatoes in vinegar.

Hannah never stopped talking and yet ate and drank enormously with little visible effect except to make him talk more loudly and more rapidly than ever.

'It was a hard school out there, believe me. You had to be good to survive and the longer you lasted, the better your chances.'

'That makes sense, I suppose,' I said.

'It sure does. You don't need luck up there, kid. You need to know what you're doing. Flying's about the most unnatural thing a man can do.'

When the waiter came to clear the table,

I thanked him. Hannah said, 'That's pretty good Portuguese you speak. Better than mine.'

'I spent a year on the lower Amazon when I first came to South America,' I told him. 'Flying out of Belem for a mining company that had diamond concessions along the Xingu River.'

He seemed impressed. 'I hear that's rough country. Some of the worst Indians in Brazil.'

'Which was why I switched to Peru. Mountain flying may be trickier, but it's a lot more fun than what you're doing.'

He said, 'You were pretty good out there today. I've been flying for better than twenty years and I can't think of more than half a dozen guys I've known who could have landed that Vega. Where did you learn to fly like that?'

'I had an uncle who was in the R.F.C.,' I said. 'Died a couple of years back. He used to take me up in a Puss Moth when I was a kid. When I went to University, I joined the Air Squadron which led to a Pilot Officer's commission in the Auxiliary Air Force. That got me plenty of weekend flying.'

'Then what?'

'Qualified for a commercial pilot's licence in my spare time, then found pilots were ten-a-penny.'

'Except in South America.'

'Exactly.' I was more than a little tight by then and yet the words seemed to spill out with no difficulty. 'All I ever wanted to do was fly. Know what I mean? I was willing to go anywhere.'

'You certainly were if you drew the Xingu. What are you going to do now? If you're stuck for a job I might be able to help.'

'Flying, you mean?'

He nodded. 'I handle the mail and general freight route to Landro which is about two hundred miles up the Negro from here. I also cover the Rio das Mortes under government contract. Lot of diamond prospecting going on up there these days.'

'The Rio das Mortes?' I said. 'The River of Death? You must be joking. That's worse than the Xingu any day. I've been there. I took some government men to a Mission Station called Santa Helena maybe two years ago. That would be before your time. You know the place?'

'I call there regularly.'

'You used a phrase today,' I said. 'The Last Place God Made. Well, that's the Rio das Mortes, Hannah. During the rainy season it never stops. At other times of the year it just rains all day. They've got flies up there that lay eggs in your eyeballs. Most parts of the Amazon would consider the *pirhana* bad enough because a shoal of them can reduce a man to a skeleton in three minutes flat, but on the Mortes, they have a microscopic item with spines that crawls up your backside given half a chance and it takes a knife to get him out again.'

'You don't need to tell me about the damn place,' he said. 'I've been there. Came in with three Hayleys and high hopes a year ago. All I've got left is the baby you arrived in today. Believe me, when my government contract's up in three months you won't see me for dust.'

'What happened to the other two planes?'

'Kaput. Lousy pilots.'

'Then why do you need me?'

'Because it takes two planes to keep my schedules going or to put it more exactly, I can't quite do it with one. I managed to pick up an old biplane the other day from a planter down-river who's selling up.'

'What is it?'

'A Bristol.'

He was in the act of filling my glass and I started so much that I spilled most of my wine across the table. 'You mean a Brisfit? A Bristol fighter? Christ, they were flying those over twenty years ago on the Western Front.'

He nodded. 'I should know. Oh, she's old all right, but then she only has to hold together another three months. Do one or two of the easy river trips. If you'd wanted the job, you could have had it, but it doesn't matter. There's a guy in at the weekend who's already been in touch with me. Some Portuguese who's been flying for a mining company in Venezuela that went bust which means I'll get him cheap.'

'Well, that's okay then,' I said.

'What are you going to do?'

'Go home – what else.'

'What about money? Can you manage?'

'Just about.' I patted my wallet. 'I won't be taking home any pot of gold, but I'll be back in one piece and that's all that counts. There's a hard time coming from what I read of events in Europe. They're going to need men with my kind of flying experience, the way things are looking.'

'The Nazis, you mean?' he nodded. 'You could be right. A bunch of bastards, from what I hear. You should meet my maintenance eingineer, Mannie Sterne. Now he's a German. Was a professor of engineering at one of their universities or something. They arrested him because he was a Jew. Put him in some kind of hell-hole they call a concentration camp. He was lucky to get out with a whole skin. Came off a freighter right here in Manaus without a penny in his pocket.'

'Which was when you met him?'

'Best day's work of my life. Where aero engines are concerned the guy's the original genius.' He re-filled my glass. 'What kind of stuff were you flying with the R.A.F. then?'

'Wapitis mainly. The Auxiliaries get the oldest aircraft.'

'The stuff the regulars don't want?'

'That's right. I've even flown Bristols.

There were still one or two around on some stations. And then there was the Mark One Fury. I got about thirty hours in one of those just before I left.'

'What's that – a fighter?' I nodded and he sighed and shook his head. 'Christ, but I envy you, kid, going back to all that. I used to be Ace-of-Aces, did you know that? Knocked out four Fockers in one morning before I went down in flames. That was my last show. Captain Samuel B. Hannah, all of twenty-three and everything but the Congressional Medal of Honour.'

'I thought that was Eddie Rickenbacker?' I said. 'Ace-of-Aces, I mean.'

'I spent the last six months of the war in hospital,' he answered.

Those blue eyes stared vacantly into the past, caught for a moment by some ancient hurt, and then he seemed to pull himself back to reality, gave me that crooked grin and raised his glass.

'Happy landings.'

The wine had ceased to effect me or so it seemed for it went down in one single easy swallow. The final bottle was empty. He called for more, then lurched across to the sliding door and pulled it back.

The music was like a blow in the face, frenetic, exciting, filling the night, mingling with the laughter, voices singing. The girl in the red satin dress moved up the steps to join him and he pulled her into his arms and she kissed him passionately. I sat there feeling curiously detached as the waiter refilled my glass and Hannah, surfacing grinned across at me.

The girl who slid into the opposite seat was part Indian to judge by the eyes that slanted up above high cheekbones. The face itself was calm and remote, framed by dark, shoulder-length hair and she wore a plain white cotton dress which buttoned down the front.

She helped herself to an empty glass and I reached for the newly opened bottle of wine and filled it for her. Hannah came across, put a hand under her chin and tilted her face. She didn't like that, I could tell by the way her eyes changed.

He said, 'You're new around here, aren't you? What's your name?'

'Maria, senhor.'

'Maria of the Angels, eh? I like that. You know me?'

'Everyone along the river knows you, senhor.'

He patted her cheek. 'Good girl. Senhor Mallory is a friend of mine – a good friend. You look after him. I'll see you're all right.'

'I would have thought the senhor well able to look after himself.'

He laughed harshly. 'You may be right, at that.' He turned and went back to the girl in the satin dress and took her down to the dance floor.

Maria of the Angels toasted me without a word and sipped a little of her wine. I emptied my glass in return, stood up and went to the rail. My head seemed to swell like a balloon. I tried breathing deeply and leaned out over the rail, letting the rain blow against my face.

I hadn't heard her move, but she was there behind me and when I turned, she put her hands lightly on my shoulders. 'You would like to dance, senhor?'

I shook my head. 'Too crowded in there.'

She turned without a word, crossed to the sliding door and closed it. The music was suddenly muted, yet plain enough a slow, sad *samba* with something of the night in it.

She came back to the rail and melted into me, one arm sliding behind my neck. Her body started to move against mine, easing me into the rhythm and I was lost, utterly and completely. A name like Maria and the face of a madonna to go with it perhaps, but the rest of her . . .

I wasn't completely certain of the sequence of things after that. The plain truth was that I was so drunk, I didn't really know what I was doing.

There was a point when I surfaced to find myself on some other part of the deck with her tight in my arms and then she was pulling away from me, telling me this was no good, that there were too many people.

She must have made the obvious suggestion – that we go to her place – because the next thing I recall is being led across that swaying catwalk to the pier.

The rain was falling harder than ever now and when we went up the steps to the pier, we ran into the full force of it. The thin cotton dress was soaked within seconds, clinging to her body, the nipples blossoming on her breasts, filling me with excitement.

I reached out for her, pulling all that ripeness into me, my hands fastening over the firm buttocks. The sap was rising with a vengeance. I kissed her pretty savagely and after a while she pushed me away and patted my face.

'God, but you're beautiful,' I said and leaned back against a stack of packing cases.

She smiled, for the first and only time I could recall in our acquaintance as if truly delighted at the compliment, a lamp turning on inside her. Then she lifted her right knee into my crotch with all her force.

I was so drunk, that I was not immediately conscious of pain, only of being down on the boardwalk, knees up to my chest.

I rolled over on my back, was aware of her on her knees beside me, hands busy in my pockets. Some basic instinct of self-preservation tried to bring me back to life when I saw the wallet in her hands, a knowledge that it contained everything of importance to me, not only material things, but my present future.

As she stood up, I reached for her ankle and got the heel of her shoe squarely in the centre of my palm. She kicked out again, sending me rolling towards the edge of the pier.

I was saved from going over by some sort of raised edging, and hung there, scrabbling for a hold frantically, no strength in me at all. She started towards me presumably to finish it off and then several things seemed to happen at once.

I heard my name, clear through the rain, saw three men halfway across the catwalk, Hannah in the lead. He had that .45 automatic in his hand and a shot echoed flatly through the rain.

Too late, for Maria of the Angels was already long gone into the darkness.

3

The Immelmann Turn

The stern-wheeler left on time the following morning, but without me. At high noon when she must have been thirty or forty miles down-river, I was sitting outside the *comandante's* office again for the second time in two days, listening to the voices droning away inside.

After a while, the outside door opened and Hannah came in. He was wearing flying clothes and looked tired, his face unshaven, the eyes hollow from lack of sleep. He'd had a contract run to make at ten o'clock, only a short hop of fifty miles or so down-river for one of the mining companies, but something that couldn't be avoided.

He sat on the edge of the sergeant's desk

and lit a cigarette, regarding me anxiously.
'How do you feel?'

'About two hundred years old.'

'God damn that bitch.' He got to his feet
and paced restlessly back and forth across
the room. 'If there was only something I could
do.' He turned to face me, really looking his
age for the first time since I'd known him. 'I
might as well level with you, kid. Every damn
thing I buy round here from fuel to booze is
on credit. The Bristol ate up all the ready
cash I had. When my government contract is
up in another three months, I'm due a reasonable enough bonus, but until then . . .'

'Look, forget about it,' I said.

'I took you to the bloody place, didn't I?'

He genuinely felt responsible, I could see
that and couldn't do much about it, a hard
thing for a man like him to accept, for his
position in other people's eyes, their opinion
was important to him.

'I'm free, white and twenty-one, isn't that
what you say in the States?' I said. 'Anything
I got, I asked for, so have a decent cigarette
for a change and shut up.'

I held out the tin of Balkan Sobranie and the door to the *comandante's* office opened and the sergeant appeared.

'You will come in now, Senhor Malllory?'

I stood up and walked into the room rather slowly which was understandable under the circumstances. Hannah simply followed me inside without asking anyone's permission.

The *comandante* nodded to him. 'Senhor Hannah.'

'Maybe there's something I can do,' Hannah said.

The *comandante* managed to look as sorrowful as only a Latin can and shook his head. 'A bad business, Senhor Mallory. You say there was a thousand *cruzeiros* in the wallet besides your passport?'

I sank into the nearest chair. 'Nearer to eleven hundred.'

'You could have had her for the night for five, senhor. To carry that kind of money on your person was extremely foolish.'

'No sign of her at all, then?' Hannah put in. 'Surely to God somebody must know the bitch.'

'You know the type, senhor. Working the river, moving from town to town. No one at *The Little Boat* had ever seen her before. She rented a room at a house near the waterfront, but had only been there three days.'

'What you're trying to say is that she's well away from Manaus by now and the chances of catching her are remote,' I said.

'Exactly, senhor. The truth is always painful. She was three-quarters Indian. She will probably go back to her people for a while. All she has to do is take off her dress. They all look the same.' He helped himself to a long black cigar from a box on his desk. 'None of which helps you. I am sensible of this. Have you funds that you can draw on?'

'Not a penny.'

'So?' He frowned. 'The passport is not so difficult. An application to the British Consul in Belem backed by a letter from me should remedy that situation within a week or two, but as the law stands at present, all foreign nationals are required to produce evidence of employment if they do not possess private means.'

I knew exactly what he meant. There were public work gangs for people like me.

Hannah moved round to the other end of the room where he could look at me and nodded briefly. He said calmly, 'No difficulty there. Senhor Mallory was considering coming to work for me anyway.'

'As a pilot?' The *comandante's* eyes went up and he turned to me. 'This is so, senhor?'

'Quite true,' I said.

Hannah grinned slightly and the *comandante* looked distinctly relieved 'All is in order then.' He stood up and held out his hand. 'If anything of interest does materialise in connection with this unfortunate affair, senhor, I'll know where to find you.'

I shook hands – it would have seemed churlish not to – and shuffled outside. I kept right on going and had reached the pillared entrance hall before Hannah caught up with me. I sat down on a marble bench in a patch of sunlight and he stood in front of me looking genuinely uncertain.

'Did I do right, back there?'

I nodded wearily. 'I'm obliged to you – really,

but what about this Portuguese you were expecting?'

'He loses, that's all.' He sat down beside me. 'Look, I know you wanted to get home, but it could be worse. You can move in with Mannie at Landro and a room at the Palace on me between trips. Your keep and a hundred dollars American a week.'

The terms were generous by any standards. I said, 'That's fine by me.'

'There's just one snag. Like I said, I'm living on credit at the moment. That means I won't have the cash to pay you till I get that government bonus at the end of my contract which means sticking out this last three months with me. Can you face that?'

'I don't have much choice, do I?'

I got up and walked out into the entrance. He said, with what sounded like genuine admiration in his voice, 'By God but you're a cool one, Mallory. Doesn't anything ever throw you?'

'Last night was last night,' I told him. 'Today's something else again. Do we fly up to Landro this afternoon?'

He stared at me, a slight frown on his face, seemed about to make some sort of comment, then obviously changed his mind.

'We ought to,' he said. 'There's the fortnightly run to the mission station at Santa Helena, to make tomorrow. There's only one thing. The Bristol ought to go, too. I want Mannie to check that engine out as soon as possible. That means both of us will have to fly. Do you feel up to it?'

'That's what I'm getting paid for,' I said and shuffled down the steps towards the cab waiting at the bottom.

The airstrip Hannah was using at Manaus at that time wasn't much. A wooden administration hut with a small tower and a row of decrepit hangar sheds backed on to the river, roofed with rusting corrugated iron. It was a derelict sort of place and the Hayley, the only aircraft on view, looked strangely out of place, its scarlet and silver trim gleaming in the afternoon sun.

It was siesta so there was no one around. I dropped my canvas grip on the ground beside the Hayley. It was so hot that I took off my flying jacket – and very still except for an occasional roar from a bull-throated howler monkey in the trees at the river's edge.

There was a sudden rumble behind and when I turned, Hannah was pushing back the sliding door on one of the sheds.

'Well, here she is,' he said.

The Bristol fighter was one of the really great combat aircraft of the war and it served overseas with the R.A.F. until well into the thirties. As I've said, there were still one or two around on odd stations in England when I was learning to fly and I'd had seven or eight hours in them.

But this one was an original – a veritable museum piece. She had a fuselage which had been patched so many times it was ridiculous and in one place, it was still possible to detect the faded rondel of the R.A.F.

Before I could make any kind of comment, Hannah said, 'Don't be put off by the state of the fuselage. She's a lot better than she looks. Structurally as sound as a bell and

I don't think there's much wrong with the engine. The guy I bought it from had her for fifteen years and didn't use her all that much. God knows what her history was before that. The log book's missing.'

'Have you flown her much?' I asked.

'Just over a hundred miles. She handled well. Didn't give me any kind of trouble at all.'

The Bristol was a two-seater. I climbed up on the lower port wing and peered into the pilot's cockpit. It had exactly the right kind of smell – a compound of leather, oil and petrol – something that had never yet failed to excite me and I reached out to touch the stick in a kind of reluctant admiration. The only modern addition was a radio which must have been fitted when the new law made them mandatory in Brazil.

'It really must be an original. Basket seat and leather cushions. All the comforts of home.'

'They were a great plane,' Hannah said soberly.

I dropped to the ground. 'Didn't I read

somewhere that van Richthofen shot down four in one day?'

'There were reasons for that. The pilot had a fixed machine-gun up front – a Vickers. The observer usually carried one or two free-mounting Lewis guns in the rear. At first, they used the usual two-seater technique.'

'Which meant the man in the rear cockpit did all the shooting?'

'Exactly, and that was no good. They sustained pretty heavy losses at first until pilots discovered she was so manoeuvrable you could fly her like a single-seater.'

'With the fixed machine-gun as the main weapon?'

'That's right. The observer's Lewis just became a useful extra. They used to carry a couple of bombs. Not much – around two hundred and forty pounds – but it means you can take a reasonable pay load. If you look, you'll see the rear cockpit has been extended at some time.'

I peered over. 'You could get a couple of passengers in there now.'

'I suppose so, but it isn't necessary. The

Hayley can handle that end of things. Let's get her outside.'

We took a wing each and pushed her out into the bright sunshine. In spite of her shabby appearance; she looked strangely menacing and exactly what she was supposed to be – a formidable fighting machine, waiting for something to happen.

'I've known people who love horses – any horse – with every fibre of their being, an instinctive response that simply cannot be denied. Aeroplanes have always affected me in exactly the same way and this was an aeroplane and a half in spite of her shabby appearance and comparatively slow speed by modern standards. There was something indefinable here that could not be stated. Of one thing I was certain – it was me she was waiting for.

Hannah said, 'You can take the Hayley. I'll follow on in this.'

I shook my head. 'No, thanks. This is what you hired me to fly.'

He looked a little dubious. 'You're sure about that?'

I didn't bother to reply, simply went and

got my canvas grip and threw it into the rear cockpit. There was a parachute in there, but I didn't bother to get it out, just pulled on my flying jacket, helmet and goggles.

He unfolded a map on the ground and we crouched beside it. The Rio das Mortes branched out of the Negro to the north-east about a hundred and fifty miles farther on. There was a military post called Forte Franco at its mouth and Landro was another fifty miles upstream.

'Stick to the river all the way,' Hannah said. 'Don't try cutting across the jungle whatever you do. Go down there and you're finished. It's Huna country all the way up the Mortes. They make those Indians you mentioned along the Xingu look like Sunday-school stuff and there's nothing they like better than getting their hands on a white man.'

'Doesn't anyone have any contacts with them?'

'Only the nuns at the medical mission at Santa Helena and it's a miracle they've survived as long as they have. One of the mining companies was having some trouble with them the other year so they called the head men of the various sub-tribes together to talk things over, then machine-gunned them from cover. Killed a couple of dozen, but they botched things up and about eight got away. Since then it's been war. It's all martial law up there. Not that it means anything. The military aren't up to much. A colonel and fifty men with two motor launches at Forte Franco and that's it.'

I folded the map and shoved it inside my flying jacket. 'From the sound of it, I'd say the Hunas have a point.'

He laughed grimly. 'You won't find many to sympathise with that statement around Landro, Mallory. They're a bunch of Stone Age savages. Vermin. If you'd seen some of the things they've done . . .'

He walked across to the Hayley, opened the cabin door and climbed inside. When he got out again, he was carrying a shotgun.

'Have you got that revolver of yours handy?' I nodded and he tossed the shotgun to me and a box of cartridges. 'Better take this as well, just in case. Best close-quarters weapon I know; 10-gauge, 6-shot automatic. The loads are double-O steel buckshot. I'd use it on myself before I let those bastards get their hands on me.'

I held it in my hands for a moment, then put it into the rear cockpit. 'Are you flying with me?'

He shook his head. 'I've got things to do. I'll follow in half an hour and still beat you there. I'll give a shout on the radio when I pass.'

There was a kind of boasting in what he said without need, for the Bristol couldn't hope to compete with the Hayley when it came to speed, but I let it pass.

Instead I said, 'Just one thing. As I remember, you need a chain of three men pulling the propeller to start the engine.'

'Not with me around.'

It was a simple statement of fact made without pride for his strength as I was soon to see, was remarkable. I stepped up on to the port wing and eased myself into that basket seat with its leather cushions and pushed my feet into the toestraps at either end of the rudder bar.

I made my cockpit checks, gave Hannah a signal and wound the starting magneto while he pulled the propeller over a compression stroke. The engine, a Rolls-Royce Falcon, exploded into life instantly.

The din was terrific, a feature of the engine at low speeds. Hannah moved out of the way and I taxied away from the hangars towards the leeward boundary of the field and turned into the wind.

I pulled down my goggles, checked the sky to make sure I wasn't threatened by anything else coming in to land and opened the throttle. Up came the tail as I pushed the stick forward just a touch, gathering speed. As she yawed to starboard in a slight cross-wind, I applied a little rudder correction. A hundred and fifty yards, a slight backward pressure on the stick and she was airborne.

At two hundred feet, I eased back the throttle to her climbing speed which was all of sixty-five miles an hour, banked steeply at five hundred feet and swooped back across the airfield.

I could see Hannah quite plainly, hands

shading his eyes from the sun as he gazed up at me. What happened then was entirely spontaneous: produced by the sheer exhilaration of being at the controls of that magnificent plane as much as by any desire to impress him.

The great German ace, Max Immelmann, came up with a brilliant ploy that gave him two shots at an enemy in a dog-fight for the price of one and without losing height. The famous Immelmann Turn, biblical knowledge for any fighter pilot.

I tried it now, diving in on Hannah, pulled up in a half-loop, rolled out on top and came back over his head at fifty feet.

He didn't move a muscle, simply stood there, shaking a fist at me. I waved back, took the Bristol low over the trees and turned up-river.

You don't need to keep your hands on a Bristol's controls at cruising speed. If you want an easy time of it, all you have to do is adjust the tailplane incidence control and sit back, but that wasn't for me. I was enjoying being in control, being at one with the machine if you like. Someone once said the Bristol was like a thoroughbred hunter with a delicate mouth and a stout heart and that afternoon over the Negro, I knew exactly what he meant.

On either side, the jungle, gigantic walls of bamboo and liana which even the sun couldn't get through. Below, the river, clouds of scarlet ibis scattering at my approach.

This was flying – how flying was meant to be and I went down to a couple of hundred feet, remembering that at that height it was possible to get maximum speed out of her. One hundred and twenty-five miles an hour. I sat back, hands steady on the stick and concentrated on getting to Landro before Hannah.

I almost made it, banking across the army post of Forte Franco at the mouth of the Rio das Mortes an hour and a quarter after leaving Manaus.

I was ten miles upstream, pushing her hard at two hundred feet when a thunderbolt descended. I didn't even know the Hayley was there until he dived on my tail, pulled up in a half-loop, rolled out on top in a perfect Immelmann Turn and roared, towards me head-on. I held the Bristol on course and he pulled up above my head.

'Bang, you're dead.' His voice crackled in my earphones. 'I was doing Immelmanns for real when you were still breast-feeding, kid. See you in Landro.'

He banked away across the jungle where he had told me not to go and roared into the distance. For a wild moment, I wondered if he might be challenging me to follow, but resisted the impulse. He'd lost two pilots already on the Mortes. No sense in making it three unless I had to.

I throttled back and continued up-river at a leisurely hundred miles an hour, whistling softly between my teeth.

4

Landro

I came to Landro, dark clouds chasing after me, the horizon closing in – another of those sudden tropical rainstorms in the offing.

It was exactly as I had expected – a clearing in the jungle at the edge of the river. A crumbling jetty, *piroques* drawn up on the beach beside it, a church surrounded by a scattering of wooden houses and not much else. In other words, a typical up-river settlement.

The landing strip was at the north end of the place, a stretch of *campo* at least three hundred yards long by a hundred across. There was a windsock on a crude pole, lifting to one side in a slight breeze and a hangar roofed with corrugated iron. Hannah was down there now with three other men, pushing the Hayley into the hangar. He turned as I came in low across the field and waved.

The Bristol had one characteristic which made a good landing difficult for the novice. The undercarriage included rubber bungees which had a catapulting effect if you landed too fast or too hard, bouncing you back into the air like a rubber ball.

I was damned if I was going to make that kind of mistake in front of Hannah. I turned down-wind for my approach. A left-hand turn, I throttled back and adjusted the tail trimmer. I glided down steadily at just on sixty, selected my landing path and turned into the wind at five hundred feet, crossing the end of the field at a hundred and fifty.

Landing speed for a Bristol is forty-five miles an hour and can be made without power if you want to. I closed the throttle, eased back the stick to flatten my glide and floated in, the only sound the wind whispering through the struts.

I moved the stick back gradually to prevent

her sinking and stalled into a perfect three-point landing, touching the ground so gently that I hardly felt a thing.

I rolled to a halt close to the hangar and sat there for a while, savouring the silence after the roar of the engine, then I pushed up my goggles and unstrapped myself. Hannah came round on the port side followed by a small, wiry man in overalls that had once been white and were now black with oil and grease.

'I told you he was good, Mannie,' Hannah said.

'You did indeed, Sam.' His companion smiled up at me.

The liking between us was immediate and mutually recognised. One of those odd occasions when you feel that you've known someone a hell of a long time.

Except for a very slight accent, his English was perfect. As I discovered later, he was fifty at that time and looked ten years older which was hardly surprising for the Nazis had imprisoned him for just over a year. He certainly didn't look like a professor. As I've said, he was small and rather insignificant, untidy, iron-grey hair falling across his forehead, the face brown and wizened. But then there were the eyes, clear grey and incredibly calm, the eyes of a man who had seen the worst life had to offer and still had faith.

'Emmanuel Sterne, Mr Mallory,' he said as I dropped to the ground.

'Neil,' I told him and held out my hand.

He smiled then, very briefly and thunder rumbled across the river, the first heavy spots of rain staining the brown earth at my feet.

'Here we go again,' Hannah said. 'Let's get this thing inside quick. I don't think this is going to be any five-minute shower.'

He gave a yell and the other two men arrived on the run. They were simply day labourers who helped out with the heavy work when needed for a pittance. Undernourished, gaunt-looking men in straw hats and ragged shirts.

There were no doors to the hangar. It was really only a roof on posts, but there was plenty of room for the Bristol beside the Hayley. We had barely got it in when the flood descended, rattling on the corrugated-iron roof like a dozen machine-guns. Outside, an impenetrable grey curtain came down between us and the river.

Mannie Sterne was standing looking at the Bristol, hands on hips. 'Beautiful,' he said. 'Really beautiful.'

'He's fallen in love again.' Hannah took down a couple of old oilskin coats from a hook and threw me one. 'I'll take you to the house. You coming, Mannie?'

Mannie was already at the engine cowling with a spanner. He shook his head without looking round. 'Later – I'll be along later.'

It was as if we had ceased to exist. Hannah shrugged and ducked out into the rain. I got my canvas grip from the observer's cockpit and ran after him.

The house was at the far end of the field, not much more than a wooden hut with a veranda and the usual corrugated iron roof. It was built on stilts as they all were, mainly because of the dampness from all that heavy rain, but also in an attempt to keep out soldier ants and other examples of jungle wildlife.

He went up the steps to the veranda and he flung open a louvred door and led the way in. The floor was plain wood with one or two Indian rugs here and there. Most of the furniture was bamboo.

'Kitchen through there,' he said. 'Shower-room next to it. There's a precipitation tank on the roof so we don't lack for a generous supply of decent water, it rains so damn much.'

'All the comforts of home,' I said.

'I would think that something of an over-statement.' He jerked his thumb at a door to the left. 'That's my room. You can share with Mannie over here.'

He opened the door, stood to one side and motioned me through. It was surprisingly large and airy, bamboo shutters open to the veranda. There were three single beds, another of those Indian rugs on the floor and there were actually some books on a shelf beside the only bed which was made up.

I picked one up and Hannah laughed shortly. 'As you can see, Mannie likes a good read. Turned Manaus upside down for that little lot.'

The book was Kant's *Critique of Pure*

Reason. I said, 'This must have been like putting his pan in the river for water and coming up with a diamond.'

'Don't tell me you go for that kind of stuff, too?' he looked genuinely put out. 'God help me, now I do need a drink.'

He went back into the living-room. I chose one of the unoccupied beds, made it up with blankets from a cupboard in the corner, then unpacked my grip. When I returned to the other room he was standing on the veranda, a glass in one hand, a bottle of Gordon's gin in the other.

The rain curtain was almost impenetrable, the first few wooden huts on their stilts at the edge of town, the only other sign of life.

'Sometimes when it gets like this, I could go crazy,' he said. 'It's as if this is all there is. As if I'm never going to get out.'

He tried to re-fill his glass, discovered the bottle was empty and threw it out into the rain with a curse. 'I need a drink. Come on – if you're not too tired I'll take you up town and show you the sights. An unforgettable experience.'

I put on my oilskin coat again and an old straw sombrero I found hanging behind the bedroom door. When I returned to the veranda he asked me if I was still carrying my revolver. As it happened, it was in one of my flying-jacket pockets.

He nodded in satisfaction. 'You'll find everybody goes armed here. It's that kind of place.'

We plunged out into the rain and moved towards the town. I think it was one of the most depressing sights I have ever seen in my life. A scabrous rash of decaying wooden huts on stilts, streets which had quickly turned into thick, glutinous mud. Filthy, ragged little children, many of them with open sores on their faces, played listlessly under the huts and on the verandas above, people stared into the rain, gaunt, hopeless, most of them trapped in that living hell for what remained of their wretched lives, no hope on earth of getting out.

The church was more substantial and included a brick and adobe tower. I commented on that and Hannah laughed shortly. 'They don't even have a regular priest. Old guy called

Father Conté who works with the nuns up at Santa Helena drops in every so often to say a Mass or two, baptise the babies and so on. He'll be coming back with us tomorrow, by the way.'

'You want me to go with you?'

'I don't see why not.' He shrugged. 'It's only a hundred-mile trip. Give you a chance to fly the Hayley. We'll have a passenger. Colonel Alberto from Forte Franco. He'll arrive about ten in the morning by boat.'

'What's he do? Some kind of regular inspection?'

'You could say that.' Hannah smiled cynically. 'The nuns up there are American. Little Sisters of Pity and very holy ladies indeed. The kind who have a mission. Know what I mean? The government's been trying to get them to move for a year or so now because of the way the Huna have been acting up, only they won't go. Alberto keeps trying, though, I'll say that for him.'

In the centre of the town, we came to the only two-storeyed building in the place. The board above the wide veranda said *Hotel* and two or three locals sat at a table without talking, staring lifelessly into space, rain blowing in on them.

'The guy who runs this place is important enough to be polite to,' Hannah observed. 'Eugenio Figueiredo. He's the government agent here so you'll be seeing a lot of him. All mail and freight has to be channelled through him for the entire upper Mortes region.'

'Are they still keen on the diamond laws as they used to be?' I asked.

'And then some. Diamond prospectors aren't allowed to work on their own up here. They have to belong to an organised group called a *garimpa* and the bossman holds a licence for all of them. Just to make sure the government gets its cut, everything they find has to be handed over to the local agent who issues a receipt and sends the loot down-river in a sealed bag. The pay-off comes later.'

'A hell of a temptation to hang on to a few.'

'And that draws you a minimum of five years in the penal colony at Machados which could fairly be described as an open grave in a swamp about three hundred miles up the Negro.'

He opened the door of the hotel and led the way in. I didn't care for the place from the start. A long, dark room with a bar down one side and a considerable number of tables and chairs. It was the smell that put me off more than anything else, compounded of stale liquor, human sweat and urine in about equal proportions and there were too many flies about for my liking.

There were only two customers. One with his back against the wall by the door, glass in hand, the same vacant look on his face as I had noticed with the men on the veranda. His companion was sprawled across the table, his straw hat on the floor, a jug overturned, its contents dribbling through the bamboo into a sizeable pool.

'*Cachaca*,' Hannah said. 'They say it rots the brain, as well as the liver, but it's all these poor bastards can afford.' He raised his voice, 'Heh, Figueiredo, what about some service.'

He unbuttoned his coat and dropped into

a basket chair by one of the open shutters. A moment later, I heard a step and a man moved through the bead curtain at the back of the bar.

Eugenio Figueiredo wasn't by any means a large man, but he was fat enough for life to be far from comfortable for him in a climate such as that one. The first time I saw him, he was shining with sweat in spite of the palm fan in his right hand which he used vigorously. His shirt clung to his body, the moisture soaking through and the stink of him was the strongest I have known in a human being.

He was somewhere in his middle years, a minor public official in spite of his responsibilities, too old for change and without the slightest hope of preferment. As much a victim of fate as anyone else in Landro. His amiability was surprising in the circumstances.

'Ah, Captain Hannah.'

An Indian woman came through the curtain behind him. He said something to her then advanced to join us.

Hannah made the introduction casually as

74

he lit a cigarette. Figueiredo extended a moist hand. 'At your orders, senhor.'

'At yours,' I murmured.

The smell was really overpowering although Hannah didn't appear in any way put out. I sat on the sill by the open shutter which helped and Figueiredo sank into a basket chair at the table.

'You are an old Brazilian hand, I think, Senhor Mallory,' he observed. 'Your Portuguese is too excellent for it to be otherwise.'

'Lately I've been in Peru,' I said. 'But before that, I did a year on the Xingu.'

'If you could survive that, you could survive anything.'

He crossed himself piously. The Indian woman arrived with a tray which she set down on the table. There was Bourbon, a bottle of some kind of spa water and three glasses.

'You will join me senhors?'

Hannah half-filled a sizeable tumbler and didn't bother with water. I took very little, in fact only drank at all as a matter of courtesy which, I think, Figueiredo was well aware of.

Hannah swallow it down and helped himself to more, staring morosely into the rain. 'Look at it,' he said. 'What a bloody place.'

It was one of those statements that didn't require any comment. The facts spoke for themselves. A group of men turned out from between two houses and trailed towards the hotel, heads down, in a kind of uniform of rubber *poncho* and straw sombrero. 'Who have we got here?' Hannah demanded.

Figueiredo leaned forward, the fan in his hand ceasing for a moment. It commenced to flutter again. '*Garimpeiros,*' he said. 'Avila's bunch. Came in last night. Lost two men in a brush with the Huna.'

Hannah poured another enormous whisky. 'From what I hear of that bastard, he probably shot them himself.'

There were five of them, as unsavoury-looking a bunch as I had ever seen. Little to choose between any of them really. The same gaunt, fleshless faces, the same touch of fever in all the eyes.

Avila was the odd man out. A big man.

Almost as large as Hannah, with a small, cruel mouth that was effeminate in its way although that was perhaps suggested more by the pencil-thin moustache which must have taken him considerable pains to cultivate.

He nodded to Figueiredo and Hannah, the eyes pausing fractionally on me, then continued to a table at the far end of the bar, his men trailing after him. When they took off their ponchos it became immediately obvious that they were all armed to the teeth and most of them carried a *machete* in a leather sheath as well as a holstered revolver.

The Indian woman went to serve them. One of them put a hand up her skirt. She didn't try to resist, simply stood there like some dumb animal while another reached up to fondle her breasts.

'Nice people,' Hannah said, although Figueiredo seemed completely unperturbed which was surprising in view of the fact that the woman, as I learned later, was his wife.

She was finally allowed to go for the drinks when Avila intervened. He lit a cigarette, produced a pack of cards and looked across at us. 'You would care to join us, gentlemen?' He spoke in quiet reasonable English. 'A few hands of poker perhaps?'

They all turned to look at us and there was a short pause. It was as if everyone waited for something to happen and there was a kind of menace in the air.

Hannah emptied his glass and stood up. 'Why not? Anything's better than nothing in this hole.'

I said, 'Not for me. I've got things to do. Another time, perhaps.'

Hannah shrugged. 'Suit yourself.'

He picked up the bottle of Bourbon and started towards the other end of the bar. Figueiredo tried to stand up, swaying so alarmingly that I moved forward quickly and took his arm.

He said softly, lips hardly moving. 'Give him an hour then come back for him on some pretence or other. He is not liked here. There could be trouble.'

The smile hooked firmly into place, he turned and went towards the others and I moved to the door. As I opened it, Avila called, 'Our company is not good enough for you, senhor?'

But I would not be drawn – not then at least, for I think that out of some strange foreknowledge, I knew that enough would come later.

When I ran out of the rain into the shelter of that primitive hangar, I found Mannie Sterne standing on a wooden platform which he had positioned at the front of the Bristol. The engine cowling had been removed and the engine was completely exposed in the light of a couple of pressure lamps he had hung overhead.

He glanced over his shoulder and smiled. 'Back so soon?'

'Hannah took me to the local pub,' I said. 'I didn't like the atmosphere.'

He turned and crouched down, a frown on his face. 'What happened?'

I gave him the whole story including Figueiredo's parting words. When I was finished, he sat there for a while, staring out into the rain. There was a sort of sadness on his face. No, more than that – worry. And there was a scar running from his right eye to the corner of his mouth. I'd failed to notice that earlier.

'Poor Sam.' He sighed. 'So, we do what Figueiredo says. We go and get him in a little while.' With an abrupt change in direction, he stood up and tapped the Bristol. 'A superb engine, Rolls-Royce. Only the best. The Bristol was one of the greatest all-purpose planes on the Western Front.'

'You were there?'

'Oh, not what you are thinking. I wasn't a Richthofen or a Udet in a skin-tight grey uniform with the blue Max at my throat, but I did visit the front-line Jagdstaffels fairly often. When I first started as an engineer, I worked for Fokker.'

'And Hannah was on the other side of the line?'

'I suppose so.'

He had returned to the engine, examining it carefully with a hand-lamp. 'This is really in excellent condition.'

I said, 'What's wrong with him? Do you know?'

'Sam?' He shrugged. 'It's simple enough. He was too good too soon. Ace-of-aces at twenty-three. All the medals in the world – all the adulation.' He leaned down for another spanner. 'But for such a man, what happens when it is all over?'

I considered the point for a while. 'I suppose in a way, the rest of his life would tend to be something of an anti-climax.'

'An understatement as far as he is concerned. Twenty years of flying mail, of barnstorming, sky-diving to provide a momentary thrill for the mindless at state fairs who hope to see his parachute fail to open, of risking his life in a hundred different ways and at the end, what does he have to show for it?' He swept his arms out in a gesture which took in everything. 'This, my friend – this is all he has and three months from now, when hiis contract ends, a government bonus of five thousand dollars.'

He looked down at me for several seconds, then turned and went back to tinkering with the engine. I didn't know what to say, but he solved the situation for me.

'You know, I'm a great believer in hunches. I go by what I think of people, instantly, in the very first moment. Now you interest me. You are your own man, a rare thing in this day and age. Tell me about yourself.'

So I did for he was the easiest man to talk to I'd ever known. He spoke only briefly himself, the odd question thrown in casually now and then, yet at the end of things, he had squeezed me dry.

He said, 'A good thing Sam was able to help you when he did, but then I'm also a great believer in fate. A man has to exist in the present moment. Accept what turns up. It's impossible to live any other way. I have a book at the house which you should read. Kant's *Critique of Pure Reason*.'

'I have done,' I said.

He turned, eyebrows raised in some surprise. 'You agree with his general thesis?'

'Not really. I don't think anything in this

life is certain enough for fixed rules to apply. You have to take what comes and do the best you can.'

'Then Heidegger is your man. I have a book of his which would interest you in which he argues that for authentic living what is necessary is the resolute confrontation of death. Tell me, were you afraid yesterday when you were attempting to land that Vega of yours?'

'Only afterwards.' I grinned. 'The rest of the time, I was too busy trying to hold the damned thing together.'

'You and Heidegger would get on famously.'

'And what would he think of Hannah?'

'Not very much, I'm afraid. Sam exists in two worlds only. The past and the future. He has never succeded in coming to terms with the present. That is his tragedy.'

'So what's left for him?'

He turned and looked at me gravely, the spanner in his right hand dripping oil. 'I only know one thing with certainty. He should have died in combat at the height of his career like so many others. At the last possible moment of the war. November 1918, for preference.'

It was a terrible thing to have to say and yet he meant it. I knew that. We stood staring at each other, the only sound the rain rushing into the ground. He wiped the oil from his hands with a piece of cotton waste and smiled sadly.

'Now I think we had better go and get him while there is still time.'

I could hear the laughter from the hotel long before we got there and it was entirely the wrong sort. I knew then we were in for trouble and so did Mannie. His face beneath the old sou'wester he wore against the rain was very pale.

As we approached the hotel steps I said, 'This man, Avila? What's he like?'

He paused in the middle of the street. 'There's a story I'm fond of about an old Hassidic Rabbi who, having no money around the house, gave one of his wife's rings to a beggar. When he told her what he'd done she went into hysterics because the ring was a family heirloom and very valuable. On hearing this, the Rabbi ran through the streets looking for the beggar.'

'To get his ring back?'

'No, to warn him of its true value in case anyone tried to cheat him when he sold it.'

I laughed out loud, puzzled. 'What's that got to do with Avila?'

'Nothing much, I suppose.' He grinned wryly. 'Except that he isn't like that.'

We turned into the alley at the side of the hotel and paused again. 'You'll find the kitchen door just round the corner as I described,' he said. 'Straight through to the bar. You can't miss it.'

There was another burst of laughter from inside. 'They seem to be enjoying themselves.'

'I've heard laughter like that before. I didn't like it then and I don't like it now. Good luck,' he added briefly and went round to the front of the hotel.

The kitchen door he had mentioned stood open and Figueiredo's wife was seated on a chair slicing vegetables into a bowl on her knee. I stepped past her, ignoring her look of astonishment and walked across the kitchen to the opposite door.

There was a short passage with the entrance to the bar at the far end and Figueiredo was standing on this side of the bead curtain peering through presumably keeping out of the way.

He glanced over his shoulder at my approach. I motioned him to silence and peered through. They were still grouped around the table, Hannah in the chair next to Avila. He was face-down across the table, quite obviously hopelessly drunk. As I watched, Avila pulled him upright by the hair, jerking the head back so that the mouth gaped.

He picked up a jug of *cachaca* and poured in about a pint. 'You like that, senhor? The wine of the country, eh?'

Hannah started to choke and Avila released him so that he fell back across the table. The rest of them seemed to find this enormously funny and one of them emptied a glass over the American's head.

There was a sudden silence as Mannie moved into view from the right. In the old sou'wester and yellow oilskin he could easily have looked ridiculous, yet didn't, which was a strange thing. He walked towards the group at the same steady pace and paused.

Avila said, 'Go away, there is nothing for you here.'

Mannie's face was paler than ever. 'Not without Captain Hannah.'

Avila's hand came up holding a revolver. He cocked it very deliberately so I produced the automatic shotgun I had been holding under my oilskin coat and shoved Figueiredo out of the way. There was a wooden post on the far side of Avila, one of several set into the floor to help support the plank ceiling. It was the kind of target that even I couldn't miss. I took careful aim and fired. The post disintegrated in the centre and part of the ceiling sagged.

I have seldom seen men scatter faster than they did and when I stepped through the bead curtain, shotgun ready, they were all flat on the floor except for Avila who crouched on one knee beside Hannah, revolver ready.

'I'd put it down if I were you,' I told him.

'This is a six-shot automatic and I'm using steel ball cartridges.'

He placed his gun very carefully on the table and stood back, eyeing me balefully. I went round the end of the bar and handed the shotgun to Mannie. Then I dropped to one knee beside Hannah, heaved him over my shoulder and stood up.

Avila said, 'I will remember this, senhors. My turn will come.'

I didn't bother to answer, simply turned and walked out and Mannie followed, the shotgun under one arm.

Hannah started to vomit halfway down the street and by the time we reached the house, there couldn't have been much left in him. We stripped him between us and got him into the shower which revived him a little, but the truth was that he was saturated with alcohol and partly out of his mind, I think, as we put him to bed.

He thrashed about for a while, hands plucking at himself. As I leaned over him, his eyes opened. He stared up at me, a slight frown on his face and smiled.

'You new, Kid? Just out from England?'

'Something like that.' I glanced at Mannie who made no sign.

'If you last a week you've got a chance.' He grabbed me by the front of my flying jacket. 'I'll give you a tip. Never cross the line alone under ten thousand feet, that's lesson number one.'

'I'll remember that,' I said.

'And the sun – watch the sun.'

I think he was trying to say more but his head fell to one side and he passed out again.

I said, 'He thought he was back on the Western Front.'

Mannie nodded. 'Always the same. Hopelessly trapped by the past.'

He tucked the blankets in around Hannah's shoulders very carefully and I went into the living-room. It had stopped raining and moisture, drawn by the heat, rose from the ground outside like smoke.

It was still cool in the bedroom and I lay

down and stared up at the ceiling, thinking about Sam Hannah, the man who had once had everything and now had nothing. And after a while, I drifted into sleep.

5

The Killing Ground

Forte Franco must have been the sort of
posting which to any career officer was equiv-
alent of a sentence of death. A sign that he
was finished. That there was no more to come.
Because of this I had expected the kind of
second-rater one usually found in command
of up-river military posts; incapable of realising
his own inadequacies and permanently soured
by his present misfortunes.

Colonel Alberto was not at all like that. I
was helping Mannie get the Hayley ready to
go when the launch came into the jetty and
he disembarked. He was every inch the soldier
in a well-tailored drill uniform, shining boots,
black polished holster on his right thigh.

Parade-ground smart and the face beneath the peaked cap was intelligent and firm although tinged with yellow as if he'd had jaundice which was a common enough complaint in the climate.

There were half a dozen soldiers in the boat, but only one accompanied him, a young sergeant as smartly turned-out as his colonel with a briefcase in one hand and a couple of machine-guns slung over one shoulder.

Alberto smiled pleasantly and spoke in quite excellent English. 'A fine morning, Senhor Sterne. Is everything ready?'

'Just about,' Mannie told him.

'And Captain Hannah?'

'Will be down shortly.'

'I see.' Alberto turned to me. 'And this gentleman?'

'Neil Mallory,' I said. 'I'm Hannah's new pilot. I'm going up with you, just to get the feel of things.'

'Excellent.' He shook hands rather formally then glanced at his watch. 'I have things to discuss with Figueiredo. I'll be back in half an hour. I'll leave Sergeant Lima here. He'll be going with us.'

He moved away, a brisk, competent figure and the sergeant opened the cabin door and got rid of the machine-guns and the briefcase.

I said to Mannie, 'What's his story? He doesn't look the type for up-country work.'

'Political influence as far as I understand it,' Mannie said. 'Said the wrong thing to some government minister or other in front of people. Something like that, anyway.'

'He looks a good man to me.'

'Oh, he's that all right. At least as far as the job is concerned, but I've never cared for the professional soldier as a type. They made the end justify the means too often for my liking.' He wiped his hands on a rag and stood back. 'Well, she's ready as she'll ever be. Better get Hannah.'

I found him in the shower, leaning in the corner for support, head turned up into the spray. When he turned it off and stepped out, he tried to smile and only succeeded in looking worse than ever.

'I feel as if they've just dug me up. What happened last night?'

'You got drunk,' I said.

'What on – wood alcohol? I haven't felt like this since Prohibition.'

He wandered off to his bedroom like a very old man and I went into the kitchen and made some coffee. When it was ready, I took it out on a tray and found him on the veranda dressed for flying.

He wrapped a white scarf around his throat and took one of the mugs. 'Smells good enough to drink. I thought you Limeys could only make tea?' He sipped a little, eyeing me speculatively. 'What really happened last night?'

'Can't you remember anything?'

'I won a little money at poker, that's for sure. More than my share and Avila and his boys weren't too happy. Was there trouble?'

'I suppose you could say that.'

'Tell me.'

So I did. There was little point in holding anything back for he was certain to hear it for himself one way or the other.

When I was finished, he sat there on the

rail holding the mug in both hands, his face very white, those pale eyes of his opaque, lifeless. As I have said, the appearance of things was of primary importance to him. His standing in other men's eyes, the image he protrayed to the world and these men had treated him like dirt – publicly humiliated him.

He smiled suddenly and unexpectedly, a slow burn as if what I had said had touched a fuse inside. I don't know what it would have done for Avila, but it certainly frightened me. He didn't say another word about the matter, didn't have to and I could only hope Avila would be long gone when we returned.

He emptied what was left of his coffee over the rail and stood up. 'Okay, let's get moving. We've got a schedule to keep.'

Flying the Hayley was like driving a car after what I'd been used to and the truth is, there wasn't much enjoyment in it. Everything worked to perfection, it was the last word in comfort and engine noise was reduced to a minimum. Hannah was beside me and Colonel Alberto sat in one of the front passenger seats, his sergeant behind to preserve, I suppose, the niceties of military rank.

Hannah opened a Thermos flask, poured coffee into two cups and passed one back. 'Still hoping to get the nuns to move on, Colonel?' he asked.

'Not really,' Alberto said. 'I raise the matter with Father Conté on each visit, usually over the sherry, because it is part of my standing orders from Army Command Headquarters. A meaningless ritual, I fear. The Church has considerable influence in government circles and at the highest possible level. No one is willing to order them to leave. The choice is theirs and they see themselves as having a plain duty to take God and modern medicine to the Indians.'

'In that order?' Hannah said and laughed for the first time that morning.

'And the Huna?' I said. 'What do they think?'

'The Huna, Senhor Mallory, want no one. Did you know what their name means in their own language? The enemy of all men. Anthropologists talk of the noble savage, but there is nothing noble about the Huna. They are probably the cruellest people on earth.'

'They were there first,' I said.

'That's what they used to say about the Sioux back home,' Hannah put in.

'An interesting comparison.' Alberto said. 'Look at the United States a century ago and look at her now. Well, this is our frontier, one of the richest undeveloped areas in the world. God alone knows how far we can go in the next fifty years, but one thing is certain – progress is inevitable and these people stand in the way of that progress.'

'So what answer have you got?' I said. 'Extermination.'

'Not if they can be persuaded to change. The choice is theirs.'

'Which gives them no choice at all.' I was surprised to hear my own bitternness.

Alberto said, 'Figueiredo was telling me you spent a year in the Xingu River country, Senhor Mallory. The Indians in that area have always been particularly troublesome. This was so when you were there?'

I nodded reluctantly.

'Did you ever kill one?'

'All right,' I said. 'I was at Forte Tomas in November thirty-six when they attacked the town and butchered thirty or forty people.'

'A bad business,' he said. 'You must have been with the survivors who took refuge in the church and held them off for a week till the military arrived. You must have killed many times during that unfortunate episode.'

'Only because they were trying to kill me.'

'Exactly.'

I could see him in my mirror as he leaned back and took a file from his briefcase, effectively putting an end to the conversation.

Hannah grinned, 'I'd say the colonel's made his point.'

'Maybe he has,' I said, 'but it still isn't going to help the Huna.'

'But why in the hell world would any sensible person want to do that?' he seemed surprised. 'They've had their day, Mallory, just like the dinosaurs.'

'Doomed to extinction, you mean?'

'Exactly.' He groaned and put a hand to

his head. 'Christ, there's someone walking around inside with hob-nailed boots.'

I gave up. Maybe they were right and I was wrong – perhaps the Huna had to go under and there was no other choice. I pushed the thought away from me, eased back the stick and climbed into the sunlight.

The whole trip took no more than forty minutes, mostly in bright sunshine although as we approached our destination we ran into another of those sudden violent rainstorms and I had to go down fast.

Visibility was temporarily so poor that Hannah took over the controls in the final stages, taking her down to two hundred feet at which height we could at least see the river. He throttled back and side-slipped neatly into the landing strip which was a large patch of *campo* on the east bank of the river.

'They don't have a radio, so I usually fly in over the settlement just to let them know I'm here,' Hannah told me. 'The nuns enjoy it, but this isn't weather to fool about in.'

'It is of no consequence,' Alberto said

calmly. 'They will have heard us land. The launch will be here soon.'

The mission, as I remembered, was a quarter of a mile up-stream on the other side of the river. Alberto told Lima to go and wait the launch's arrival and produced a leather cigar case.

Hannah took one, but I declined and on impulse, opened the cabin door and jumped down into the grass. The rain hammered down relentlessly as I went after the sergeant. There was a crude wooden pier constructed of rough-hewn planks, extending into the river on piles, perhaps twenty or thirty feet long.

Lima was already at the end. He stood there, gazing out across the river. Suddenly he leaned over the edge of the jetty, dropping to one knee as if looking down at something in the water. As I approached, he stood up, turned to one side and was violently sick.

'What's wrong?' I demanded, then looked over the edge and saw for myself. I took several deep breaths and said, 'You'd better get the colonel.'

An old canoe was tied up to the jetty and the thing which floated beside it, trapped by the current against the pilings was dressed in the tropical-white robes of a nun. There was still a little flesh on the skeletal face that stared out from the white coif, but not much. A sudden eddy pulled the body away. It rolled over, face-down and I saw there were at least half a dozen arrows in the back.

Lima climbed up out of the water clutching an identity disc and crucifix on a chain which he'd taken from around the nun's neck. He looked sicker than ever as he handed them to Alberto and stood there shaking and not only from the cold.

Alberto said, 'Pull yourself together for God's sake and try and remember you're a soldier. You're safe enough here anyway. I've never known them to operate on this side of the river.'

If we'd done the sensible thing we'd have climbed back into the Hayley and got to hell out of there. Needless to say, Alberto didn't consider that for a second. He stood at the end of the jetty peering into the rain, a machine-gun cradled in his left arm.

'Don't tell me you're thinking of going across?' Hannah demanded.

'I have no choice. I must find out what the situation is over there. There could be survivors.'

'You've got to be joking,' Hannah exploded angrily. 'Do I have to spell it out for you? It's finally happened, just as every-one knew it would if they didn't get out of there.'

Colonel Alberto ignored him and said, without turning round, 'I would take it as a favour if you would accompany me Senhor Mallory. Sergeant Lima can stay here with Senhor Hannah.'

Hannah jumped in with both feet, his ego, I suppose, unable to accept the fact of being left behind. 'To hell with that for a game of soldiers. If he goes, I go.'

I don't know if it was the result Alberto had intended, but he certainly didn't argue. Sergeant Lima was left to hold the fort with his revolver, I took the other machine-gun and Hannah had the automatic shotgun he habitually carried in the Hayley.

There was water in the canoe. It swirled about in the bottom breaking over my feet in little waves as I sat in the stern and paddled. Hannah was in the centre, also paddling and Alberto crouched in the prow, his machine-gun at the ready.

An old log, drifting by, turned into an alligator by flicking his tail and moving lazily out of the way. The jungle was quiet in the rain, the distant cough of a jaguar the only sound. On the far side of the river, sandbanks lifted out of the water, covered with *ibis* and as we approached, thousands of them lifted into the rain in a great, red cloud.

The sandbanks appeared and disappeared at intervals for most of the way, finally rising in a shoal a good two hundred yards long in the centre of the river opposite the mission jetty.

'I landed and took off from there twice last year during the summer when the river was low,' Hannah said.

I suspected he had made the remark for something to say more than anything else for we were drifting in towards the jetty now and the silence was uncanny.

We tied up alongside an old steam launch and climbed up on to the jetty. A couple of wild dogs were fighting over something on the ground at the far end. They cleared off as we approached. When we got close, we saw it was another nun, lying face-down, hands hooked into the dirt.

Flies rose in clouds at our approach and the smell was frightful. Alberto held a handkerchief to his face and dropped to one knee to examine the body. He slid his hand underneath, groped around for a while and finlly came up with the identity disc he was seeking on its chain. He stood up and moved away hurriedly to breathe fresh air.

'Back of her skull crushed, probably by a war club.'

'How long?' Hannah asked him.

'Two days – three at the most. If there has been a general massacre then we couldn't be safer. They believe the spirits of those killed violently linger in the vicinity for seven days. There isn't a Huna alive who'd come anywhere near this place.'

I don't know whether his words were

supposed to reassure, but they certainly didn't do much for me. I slipped the safety catch off the machine-gun and held it at the ready as we went forward.

The mission itself was perhaps a hundred yards from the jetty. One large single-storeyed building that was the medical centre and hospital, four simple bungalows with thatched roofs and a small church on a rise at the edge of the jungle and close to the river, a bell hanging from a frame above the door.

We found two more nuns before we reached the mission, both virtually hacked to pieces, but the most appalling sight was at the edge of the clearing at the end of the medical centre where we discovered the body of a man suspended by his ankles above the cold ashes of what had been a considerable fire, the flesh peeling from his skull. The smell was nauseating, so bad that I could almost taste it.

Alberto beat the flies away with a stick and took a close look. 'Father Conté's servant,' he said. 'An Indian from down-river. Poor devil, they must have decided he'd earned something special.'

Hannah turned on me, his face like the wrath of God. 'And you were feeling sorry for the bastards.'

Colonel Alberto cut in quickly. 'Never mind that now. Your private differences can wait till later. We'll split up to save time and don't forget I need identity bracelets. Another day in this heat and it will be impossible to recognise anyone.

I took the medical centre, an eerie experience because everything was in perfect order. Beds turned down as if awaiting patients, mosquito nets hooked up neatly. The only unusual thing was the smell which led me to the small operating theatre where I found two more nuns, their bodies already decomposing. Like the one at the end of the jetty they seemed to have been clubbed to death. I managed to find their identity discs without too much trouble and got out.

Alberto was emerging from one of the bungalows. I gave him the discs and he said, 'That makes ten in all; there should be a dozen. And there's no sign of Father Conté.'

'All they've done is kill people,' I said.

'Everything else is in perfect order. It doesn't make sense. I'd have expected them to put a torch to the buildings, just to finish things off.'

'They wouldn't dare,' he said. 'Another superstition. The spirits of those they have killed need somewhere to live.'

Hannah moved out of the church and called to us. When we joined him he was shaking with rage. Father Conté lay flat on his back just inside the door, an arrow in his throat. From his position, I'd say he had probably been standing on the porch facing his attackers when hit. His eyes had gone, probably one of the vultures which I had noticed perched on the church roof. Most terrible thing of all, his cassock had been torn away and his chest hacked open with a *machete*.

Hannah said, 'Now why would they do a thing like that?'

'They admired his courage. They imagine that by eating his heart, they take some of his bravery into themselves.'

Which just about finished Hannah off and he looked capable of anything as Alberto said, 'There are two nuns missing. We know they're not inside anywhere so we'll split up again and work our way down through the mission in a rough line. They're probably face-down in the grass somewhere.'

But they weren't, or at least we couldn't find them. When we gathered again at the jetty, Hannah said, 'Maybe they went into the water like the first one we found?'

'All the others were either in their middle years or older,' Alberto said. These two, the two who are missing, are much younger than that. Twenty or twenty-one. No more.'

'You think they've been taken alive?' I asked him.

'It could well be. Like many tribes, they like to freshen the blood occasionally. They frequently take in young women, keep them until the baby is born then murder them.'

'For God's sake, let's get out of here,' Hannah said. 'I've had about all I can take.' He turned and hurried to the end of the jetty and boarded the canoe.

There wasn't much more we could do anyway so we joined him and paddled back downstream. The journey was completely uneventful. When we drifted in to the jetty at the edge of the *campo*, Lima was waiting for us looking more nervous than ever.

'Everything all right here?' Alberto demanded.

Lima said anxiously, 'I don't know, Colonel.' He nodded towards the green curtain of jungle. 'You know what it's like. You keep imagining that someone is standing on the other side, watching you.'

Forest foxes started to bark in several different directions at once. Alberto said calmly, 'I suggest we walk back to the plane quietly and get inside with the minimum of fuss. I think we're being watched.'

'The foxes?' I said.

'Aren't foxes – not at this time in the morning.'

The walk to the plane was an experience in itself and I expected an arrow in the back at any moment. But nothing happened. We all got inside without incident and I took the controls.

I taxied to the end of the *campo*. As I turned

into the wind, an Indian emerged from the jungle and stood on the edge of the clearing watching us, face painted for war, magnificent in a head-dress of parrot feathers, a spear in one hand, a six-foot bow in the other.

Hannah picked up one of the machine-guns and reached for the window. Alberto caught his arm. 'No, leave it. Our turn will come.'

As we moved past, another figure emerged from the forest, then another and another. I don't think I have ever felt happier than when I lifted the Hayley over the trees at the edge of the *campo*, stamped on the rudder and swung north.

There was no landing strip at Forte Franco for the simple reason that the post had been built on an island strategically situated at the mouth of the Negro about a century before the Wright brothers first left the ground.

We radioed the bad news ahead the moment we were in range, just to get things moving, then put down at Landro. Alberto wasted little time in getting under way. He ordered his men to prepare the launch for a quick departure then went into Landro with Hannah to see Figueiredo. I was waiting at the jetty with Mannie when the colonel returned. Hannah was not with him.

'What happens now?' I asked.

'There should be a reply to my message from Army Headquarters by the time I reach Forte Franco. I would imagine my instructions will be to proceed up-river at once with my command. All thirty-eight of them. 'I've a dozen men down with fever at the moment.'

'But surely they'll send you reinforcements?' Mannie said.

'Miracles sometimes happen, but not very often, my friend. Even if they did, it would be several weeks before they could arrive. This kind of thing is an old story as you must know, Senhor Mallory.' He looked out across the river to the forest. 'In any case, in that kind of country, a regiment would be too little, an army not enough.'

'When we landed, you said we'd be safe on that side of the river,' I reminded him. 'That they never crossed over.'

He nodded, his face dark and serious. 'A cause for concern, I assure you, if it means they are moving out of their usual territory.' The engine of the launch broke into life and he smiled briskly. 'I must be on the move. Senhor Hannah stayed at the hotel, by the way. I'm afraid he has taken all this very hard.'

He stepped over the rail, one of the soldiers cast off and the launch moved into midstream. We stood watching it go. Alberto waved, then went into the cabin.

I said, 'What about Hannah? Do you think there's any point in going for him? If he runs into Avila in the mood he's in . . .'

'Avila and his bunch moved out just before noon.' Mannie shook his head. 'Best leave him for now. We can put him to bed later.'

He turned and walked away. A solitary ibis hovered above the trees on the other side of the river before descending like a splash of blood against the grey sky. An omen, perhaps, of worse things to come?

I shivered involuntarily and went after Mannie.

6

The Scarlet Flower

In the days which followed the news from up-river wasn't good. Several rubber tappers were killed and a party of diamond prospectors, five in all, died to the last man in an ambush not ten miles above the mission.

Alberto and his men, operating out of Santa Helena, didn't seem to be accomplishing much, which wasn't really surprising. If they kept to the tracks the Huna ambushed them and if they tried to hack a way through the jungle, their progress was about one mile a day to nowhere.

In a week, he'd lost seven men. Two dead, three wounded and two injured, one by what was supposed to be an accidental cut on the leg with a *machete* which sounded more as if it had been self-inflicted to me. I saw the man involved when Hannah, who was flying him out to Manaus, dropped in at Landro to refuel and I can only say that considering his undoubted pain, he seemed remarkably cheerful.

Hannah was making a daily trip to Santa Helena under the circumstances which left me with the Landro-Manaus mail run in the Bristol. The general attitude in Manaus was interesting. Events up-river might have been taking place on another planet as far as they were concerned, and even in Landro no one seemed particularly excited.

Two things changed that. The first was the arrival of Avila and his bunch – or what was left of them – one evening just before dark. They all seemed to have sustained minor wounds of one sort or another and had lost two men in an ambush on a tributary of the Mortes on the side of the river where the Huna weren't supposed to be.

Even then, people didn't get too worked up. After all, Indians had been killing the odd white up-country for years. It was only when the boat drifted in with the two dead on board that the harsh reality was really brought home.

It was a nasty business. Mannie found them early on Sunday morning when he was taking a walk before breakfast and sent one of the labourers for me. By the time I got there people were already hurrying along to the jetty in twos and threes.

The canoe had grounded on the sandbank above the jetty, pushed by the current. The occupants, as was discovered later from their papers, were rubber tappers and were feathered with more arrows than I would have believed possible.

They had been dead for at least three days and were in the condition you would have expected considering the climate, flies buzzing around in clouds and the usual smell. There was one rather nasty extra. The man in the stern had fallen backwards, one arm trailing in the water and the *piranha* had taken the flesh from his bones up to the elbow.

No one was particularly cheerful after

that and they clustered in small groups, talking in low voices until Figueiredo arrived and took charge of things. He stood there leaning on his stick, face sombre, the sweat soaking through shirt and linen jacket and watched as half a dozen labourers with handkerchiefs around their faces got the bodies out.

The Huna bows were six feet in length, taller than the men who used them and so powerful that an arrow taken in the chest frequently penetrated the entire body, the head protruding from the back. They were usually tipped with *piranha* teeth or razor-sharp bamboo.

A labourer pulled one out of one of the corpses and handed it to Figueiredo. He examined it briefly then snapped it in his two hands and threw the pieces away angrily.

'Animals!' he said. 'They'll be coming out of the jungle next.'

Which started the crowd off nicely. They wanted blood, that much was evident. The Huna were vermin and there was only one way to handle vermin. Extermination. The voices buzzed around me. I listened for a while, then turned, sick to the stomach, and walked away.

I was helping myself to a large Scotch from Hannah's private stock when Mannie came in. 'That bad?' he said calmly.

'Everywhere you go, the same story,' I said. 'It's always the Indians' fault – never the whites.'

He lit one of those foul-smelling Brazilian cigars he favoured and sat on the veranda rail. 'You feel pretty strongly about all this. Most people would think that strange in someone who was at Forte Tomas. Who came as close to being butchered by Indians as a man can get.'

'If you reduce men to symbols, then killing them is easy,' I said. 'An abstraction. Kill a Huna and you're not killing an individual – you're killing an Indian. Does that make any kind of sense to you?'

He was obviously deeply moved and at a distance of years knowing in detail what was even then happening to his people, I suppose the plain truth was that I was hitting close to home.

He said, 'A profound discovery to make so early in life. May I ask how?'

There was no reason not to speak of it although the tightness was there in the chest the moment I began, the constricted breathing. An unutterable feeling of having lost something worth having.

'It's simple,' I said. 'In my first month on the Xingu I met the best man I'm ever likely to see if I live to be a hundred. If he'd been a Catholic, they'd have tossed a coin to decide between burning or canonising him.'

'Who was he?'

'A Viennese named Karl Buber. He came out here as a young Lutheran pastor to join a mission on the Xingu. He threw it all up in disgust when he discovered the unpalatable fact that the Indians were suffering as much at the hands of the missionaries as of anyone else.'

'What did he do?'

'Set up his own place up-river from Forte Tomas, Dedicated his life to working amongst the Civa and they could teach the Huna a thing or two, believe me. He even married one. I used to fly him stuff up from Belem without the company knowing. He was the best friend the Civa ever had.'

'And they killed him?'

I nodded. 'His wife told him her father was desperately wounded and in urgent need of medical attention after the Forte Tomas attack. When Buber got there, they clubbed him to death.'

Mannie frowned slightly as if not quite understanding. 'You mean his own wife betrayed him?'

'She did it for the tribe,' I said. 'They admired Buber for his courage and wisdom. They killed him as Father Conté was killed at Santa Helena, that their chiefs might have his brains and heart.'

There was genuine horror on his face now. 'And you can still think kindly of such people?'

'Karl Buber would have. If he were here now, he'd tell you that the Indian is as much a product of his environment as a jaguar.

That he only survives in that green hell out there across the river by being willing to kill instinctually, without a moment's thought, several times a day. Killing is part of his nature.'

'Which includes killing his friends?'

'He doesn't have any. He has his blood ties – family and tribe. Anyone else is outside and on borrowed time. Ripe for the block sooner or later as Buber discovered.'

I poured another whisky. Mannie said, 'And what is your personal solution to the problem?'

'There isn't one,' I said. 'There's too much here worth the having. Diamonds in the rivers, every kind of mineral ever heard of and probably a few we haven't. Now what man worth his salt would let a bunch of Stone-Age savages stand between him and a slice of that kind of cake?'

He smiled sadly and put a hand on my shoulder. 'A dirty world, my friend.'

'And I've had too much to drink considering the time of day.'

'Exactly. Go have a shower and I'll make some coffee.'

I did as he suggested, sluicing myself in lukewarm water for ten minutes or so. As I was dressing, there was a knock at the door and Figueiredo stuck his head in.

'A bad business.' He sank into the nearest chair, mopping his face with a handkerchief. 'I've just been on the radio to Santa Helena, giving Alberto the good news.'

The military had installed a much more powerful radio transmitter and receiving unit than his in the hangar and had left a young corporal to man it.

'Hannah stayed up there overnight,' I said as I pulled on my flying jacket. 'Any word from him?'

Figueiredo nodded. 'He wants you to join him as soon as possible.'

'At Santa Helena?' I shook my head. 'You must have got it wrong. I've got the mail run to make to Manaus.'

'Cancelled. You're needed on military business which takes precedence.'

'Well, that's intriguing,' I said. 'Any idea what it's all about?'

He shook his head. 'Not my business to

know. Where military affairs are concerned, I have no jurisdiction at all and what's more, I like it that way.'

Mannie kicked open the door and came in with coffee in two tin cups. 'You've heard?' I said.

He nodded. 'I'd better get across to the hangar and get the Bristol ready to move.'

I stood at the window beside Figueiredo, sipping my coffee, gazing down towards the jetty. A cart came towards us, pulled by a couple of half-starved oxen, a collection of moving bones held together by a bag of skin. The driver kept them going by sticking a six-inch nail on the end of a pole beneath their tails at frequent intervals.

As the cart went by, the smell told us what was inside. Figueiredo turned, an expression of acute distaste on his face. He opened his mouth to speak and the rain came down in a sudden rush, rattling on the corrugated-iron roof, drowning all sound.

We stood there together and watched the cart disappear into the gloom.

* * *

It was still raining when I took off, not that I was going to let that put me off. The massacre of Santa Helena had been worse, but the two poor wretches in the canoe had brought a whiff of the open grave with them, a touch of unease, a feeling that something waited out there in the trees across the river. Landro was definitely a place to put behind you on such a morning.

I followed the river all the way and seeing no reason to push hard, especially once I ran out of the rain, took a good hour over getting there, giving myself time to enjoy the flight.

I went in low over Santa Helena itself, just to see how things stood. The mission launch was just leaving the jetty and moving down-river, but the old forty-foot military gunboat was still there. A couple of soldiers moved out of the hospital and waved and Hannah came out of the priest's house. I circled again, then cut across the river and dropped into the airstrip.

There was a permanent guard of ten men with two heavy machine-guns. The sergeant in charge detailed one man to take me up to

Santa Helena in a dinghy powered by an outboard motor.

Hannah was waiting at the end of the jetty, smoking a cigarette. 'You took your own sweet time about getting here,' he commented sourly.

'Nobody told me there was any rush,' I said as I scrambled up on to the jetty. 'What's it all about anyway?'

'We're going to drop a few Christmas presents into your friends the Huna,' he said.

He had a couple of large sacks with him which he handed to the soldier in the boat. He went down the ladder and cast off. 'I'll send him back for you. I've got things to do. You'll find Alberto at the priest's house. He'll fill you in.'

He sat down in the prow, lighting another of his interminable cigarettes and shoved his hands into the pockets of his leather coat, looking about as fed-up as it was possible to be.

I was completely mystified by the whole affair and keen for an early explanation, so I turned away and hurried along the jetty.

There was a sentry at the land end who looked bored and unhappy, sweat soaking through his drill tunic. There were two more beside a machine-gun in the church porch.

I found Alberto in the priests's house. He was lying on a narrow bed, minus his breeches, his right leg supported across a pillow while his medical corporal swabbed away at a couple of leg ulcers with cotton wool and iodine. Alberto, who looked anything but happy, was obtaining what solace he could from the glass in his left hand and the bottle of brandy in his right.

'Ah, Senhor Mallory,' he said. 'I would not wish these things on my worst enemy. Like acid, they eat right through to the bone.'

'Better than having them on your privates.'

He smiled grimly. 'A sobering thought. Has Captain Hannah explained things to you?'

'He said something unintelligible about Christmas presents for the Huna, then took off across river. What's it all about?'

'It's simple enough. I've managed to lay hands on a half-breed who's been living with them. He's fixed the position of their main village for me on the map. About forty miles into the bush from here.'

'You're going to attack?'

He groaned aloud and moved restlessly under the corporal's hand, sweat beading his forehead. 'An impossibility. It would take us at least three weeks to force a way through even if my man agreed to lead us which he would certainly refuse to do under those circumstances. It would be suicide. They'd pick us off one by one.'

'What about reinforcements?'

'There aren't any. They're having trouble with the Civa along the Xingu again and the Jicaro are making things more than difficult along their stretch of the Negro. My orders are to come to some sort of terms with the Huna, then to abandon Santa Helena. I've just sent the mission launch down to Landro with everything on board worth saving.'

'And why am I here?'

'I want you to fly to this Huna village with Hannah. Drop in a couple of sackfuls of trade goods of various kinds, as a gesture of good-will. Then I'll send in this man who's been living with them to try and arrange a meeting for me.'

He reached for a clean glass as the sergeant started to bandage his leg, half-filled it with brandy and passed it across to me. I didn't really want it, but took it out of politeness.

He said, 'I've been making inquiries about you, Mallory. You were friendly with that madman Buber when you were on the Xingu. Probably know more about Indians than I do. What kind of chance do you think my plan has of working?'

'Not a hope,' I said. 'If you want the truth, that is.'

'I agree entirely.' He toasted me then emptied his glass. 'But at least I'll have made the kind of positive step to do something that even Headquarters won't be able to quarrel with.'

I tried the brandy which tasted as if someone had made it in the bath. I placed the glass down carefully. 'I'll be off then. Presumably Hannah is straining at the leash.'

'He isn't too pleased, I can tell you that.' Alberto reached across and picked up my glass. 'Safe journey.'

I left him there and went out into bright sunlight again. The heat was terrific, dust rising from the dry earth with each step, and the jungle was already beginning to creep in at the back of the hospital, lianas trailing in across the roof from the trees. It didn't take long. People came and went, but the forest endured, covering the scars they left as if they had never existed.

The dinghy was waiting and had me back across at the landing strip in a quarter of an hour. I found Hannah lying in the shade of the Hayley's port wing, studying a map. He was as bad-tempered and morose as ever.

'Well, what do you think?' he demanded impatiently.

'A waste of time.'

'Exactly what I told him, but he will have it.' He got to his feet. 'Have a look at that. I've marked a course although the bloody place probably won't exist when we get there.'

'You want me to fly her?'

'That's what I pay you for, isn't it?'

He turned and climbed up into the cabin. Strange, in view of what happened afterwards, but I think it was at that precise moment in time that I started to actively dislike him.

I flew at a thousand feet and conditions were excellent, the sun so bright that I had to wear dark glasses. Hannah was directly behind me in the front passenger seat beside the rear door. He didn't say a word, simply sat there scanning the jungle below with a pair of binoculars.

Not that it was really necessary. No more than fifteen minutes after leaving the airstrip we passed over a large clearing and I went down to five hundred and circled it a couple of times.

'Wild banana plantation,' Hannah said. 'We're dead on course. Must be.'

Most forest Indians engaged in a crude form of husbandry when clearings such as the one below allowed it and it was an infallible sign that we were close to a large village.

I flew on, staying at five hundred feet and almost immediately felt Hannah's hand on my shoulder. 'We're here.'

The clearing seemed to flower out of the

jungle beneath my port wing. It was larger than I had expected, fifty yards in diameter at least, the thatched long huts arranged in a neat circle around a central space with some sort of tribal totem in the centre.

There must have been two hundred people down there, perhaps three, scurrying from the huts like brown ants, faces turned up as I went in across the clearing at three hundred feet. No one ran for the forest for they were familiar enough with aeroplanes, I suppose, to realise we couldn't land. Many of the warriors actually loosed off arrows at us.

'Stupid bastards. Would you look at that now?' Hannah laughed harshly. 'Okay, kid, let's get it over with. Take her in at a hundred feet, slow as you like.'

I banked to starboard, throttled back and went down across the trees. Hannah had the door open, I was aware of the wind and then the village was directly in front, faces upturned, arrows arching up towards us impotently.

I eased back the stick to climb, glancing over my shoulder in time to see a ball of fire explode in the centre of the crowd closely followed by another.

I saw worse things in the war that was to come, far worse, and yet it haunts me still.

I should have known, I suppose, expected it at least, yet it's easy to be wise after the event. He was laughing like a madman as I took the Hayley round again and went in through the smoke.

There were bodies everywhere, dozens of them, a large central crater and the thatched roofs of several of the long-huts had caught fire.

I glanced over my shoulder. Hannah was leaning out of the open door and laughed out loud again. 'How do you like that, you bastards?' he yelled.

I struck out wildly at him backwards with one hand. The Hayley lurched to one side, faltered, then the nose went down. We grabbed at the stick together, pulling her out with no more than three hundred feet in it and it took the two of us to do it.

I levelled off and started to climb. He took his hands off mine and dropped back into his seat. Neither of us said a word and as I turned back across the clearing for the last time, flames blossomed into a scarlet flower in the clear air.

I was numb, I suppose, from the horror of it all for the next coherent thing I remember is coming in to land at the airstrip at Santa Helena. I wasn't aware of anything very much except the Bristol at the south end. I went in that way which gave me the whole of the strip to play with and rolled to a halt about forty yards from the trees.

I sat there in the silence after cutting the engine, my hands shaking, mouth dry, teeth clenched together in a kind of rictus, aware that Hannah had opened the rear door and had got out. When I opened mine, he was standing below lighting a cigarette in cupped hands.

He looked up and grinned, 'It's always rough the first time, kid.'

The grin was a mistake. I jumped straight at him and put my fist into it at the same time. We milled around there on the floor for a while, my hands at his throat and in spite of his enormous strength, I didn't do too badly, mainly because surprise was on my side. I was aware of voices shouting, men running and then several different hands grabbed me at once and dragged me off him.

They clammed me hard up against the side of the Hayley, a sergeant holding the barrel of a revolver under my chin and then Colonel Alberto arrived. He waved the man with the revolver away and looked me straight in the eye.

'It would pain me to have to arrest you, Senhor Mallory, but I will do so if necessary. You will please remember that military law only applies in this area. I am in sole command.

'God damn you!' I said. 'Don't you realise what this swine's just done? He's killed at least fifty people and I helped him do it.'

Alberto turned to Hannah and produced a cigarette case from his tunic pocket which he offered to him. 'It worked then?'

'Like a charm,' Hannah told him, and took a cigarette.

Alberto actually offered me one. I took it mechanically. 'You know?'

'I was in a difficult situation, Senhor Mallory. I needed both of you to do the thing successfully and it did not seem likely, in view of the sentiments you expressed at our last meeting, that you would give your services willingly.'

'You've made me an accessory to murder.'

He shook his head and answered gravely, 'A military operation from start to finish and fully authorised by my superiors.'

'You lied to me,' I said. 'About wanting to talk with the Huna.'

'Not at all. Only now, having shown that we mean business, that we can hit them hard when we want to, I can talk from a position of strength. You and Captain Hannah may very well prove to have been instrumental in bringing an end to this whole sorry business.'

'By butchering poor, bloody savages with high explosives dropped from the air.'

They stood around me in a semi-circle, the soldiers, few of them understanding for we spoke in English.

Hannah was quieter now, his face white and strained. 'For God's sake, Mallory, what about the nuns? Look what they did to Father Conté. They ate his heart, Mallory. They cut out his heart and ate it.'

My voice seemed to come from outside me and I was someone else inside my head, listening to me talking. I said patiently, genuinely wanting him to understand, or so it seemed to me, 'And what good does it do to act just as barbarically in return?'

It was Alberto who answered. 'You have a strange morality, Senhor Mallory. For the Huna to rape and butcher the nuns, to roast men over a fire is acceptable. For my men to die in ambush out there in the forest is all part of some game for which you apparently can accept rules.'

'Now you're twisting it. Making it something else.'

'I don't think so. You would allow us to shoot them in a skirmish in the bush, but to kill them with dynamite from the air is different . . .'

I couldn't think of anything to say for by

then, reaction had set in and I was hopelessly confused.

'A bullet in the belly, an arrow in the back, a stick of dynamite from the air.' He shook his head. 'There are no rules, Senhor Mallory. This is a dirty business. War has always been thus and this is war, believe me . . .'

I turned and walked away from them towards the Bristol. When I reached it, I leaned on the lower port wing for a while, then I took my flying helmet and goggles from one pocket of my leather jacket and put them on.

When I turned, I found Hannah standing watching me. I said, 'I'm getting out as soon as I get back. You can find someone else.'

He said tonelessly, 'We've got a contract, kid, with your signature on the bottom under mine and legally enforceable.'

I didn't say anything, simply climbed in and went through the fifteen checks, then I wound the starting magneto. Hannah pulled the propeller over, the engine clattered into life and I started to move forward so quickly that he had to duck under the lower port wing.

His face was very white, I remember that and his mouth opening and closing as he shouted to me, but his words were drowned by the roar of the Falcon engine and I didn't wait to hear, didn't care if I never clapped eyes on him again.

I was not really aware of having been asleep, only of being shaken roughly awake. I lay there staring up through the mosquito net at the pressure lamp on its hook in the ceiling, moths clustering thickly around it. The hand shook me again, I turned and found Mannie at my side.

'What time is it?' I asked him.

'Just after midnight.' He was wearing his yellow oilskin coat and sou'wester and they ran with moisture. 'You'll have to help me with Sam, Neil.'

It took a moment for it to sink in. I said, 'You've got to be joking,' and turned over.

He had me half-up by the front of the cotton shirt I was wearing with a grip of surprising strength. 'When I left he was just finishing his second bottle of brandy and

137

calling for number three. He'll kill himself unless we help him.'

'And you really expect me to give a damn after what he did to me today?'

'Now that's interesting. You said what he did to you, not what he did to those poor bloody savages out there in the bush. Which is most important?'

It almost made my hair stand up on my head in horror at what he was suggesting. I said, 'For God's sake, Mannie.'

'All right, you want him to die, then?'

I got out of bed and started to dress. I'd gone through the whole sorry story with Mannie as soon as I'd got back. Had to get it off my chest before I went mad. What I was looking for, I think, was the reassurance which would come from finding someone else who was just as horrified as I was myself.

His attitude hadn't been entirely satisfactory and he'd seemed to see rather more in Colonel Alberto's argument than I was prepared to accept myself. The strange thing was that he seemed worried about Hannah who had avoided me completely since he'd flown in.

I'd washed my hands of both of them, had helped myself to far more of Hannah's Scotch than was good for me and my head ached from it all as I went up the main street through the rain at Mannie's side.

I could hear music from the hotel as we approached and light filtered out through the shutters in golden bars. There was the sound of a glass breaking and someone called out.

We paused on the veranda and I said, 'If he decides to go berserk, he could probably break the two of us in his bare hands. I hope you realise that.'

'You're the devil himself for looking on the black side of things.' He smiled and put a hand on my arm for a moment. 'Now let's have him out of here while there's still hope.'

There were two or three people at the far end of the room, Figueiredo behind the bar and Hannah propped up against it in front of him. An old phonograph was playing *Valse Triste*, Figueiredo's wife standing beside it.

'More, more!' Hannah shouted, pounding

on the bar with the flat of his hand as the music started to run down.

She wound the handle vigorously and Hannah reached for the half-empty bottle of brandy and tried to fill the tumbler at his elbow, sending a couple of dirty glasses crashing to the floor at the same moment.

He failed to notice our approach until Mannie reached over and firmly took the bottle from his hand. 'Enough is enough, Sam. Now I think we go home.'

'Good old Mannie.' Hannah patted him on the cheek then turned to empty his glass and saw me. God, he was drunk, his face swollen with the stuff, the hands shaking and the look in his eyes . . .

He took me by the front of the coat and said wildly, 'You think I wanted to do that back there? You think it was easy?'

The man was in hell or so it seemed to me then. Certainly enough to make me feel sorry for him. I pulled free and said gently, 'Let's get you to bed then, Sam.'

Behind me the door opened, there was a

burst of careless laughter, then silence. Hannah's eyes widened and hot rage flared. He brushed me aside and plunged forward and I turned in time to see him give Avila his fist full in the mouth.

'I'll teach you, you bastard,' he yelled and pushed Avila back across a table with one hand while he pounded away at him with the other.

Avila's friends were already running into darkness which left Mannie and me. God knows, it took everything we had for I think it was himself Hannah was trying to beat to death there across the table and his strength was incredible.

As we got him out through the door, he turned and grabbed at me again. 'You won't leave me, kid, will you? We've got a contract. You gave me your word. It means everything – everything I've got in the world.'

I didn't need the look on Mannie's face, but it helped. I said soothingly, 'How can I leave, Sam? I've got the mail run to Manaus at nine a.m.'

He broke down completely at that, great sobs racking his body as we took him down the steps between us into the rain and started home.

7

Sister of Pity

I didn't see anything of Hannah on the following morning. When I took off for Manaus at nine, he was still dead to the world and Mondays were usually busy so I didn't have time to hang around.

There was not only the mail but a parcel of diamonds from Figueiredo in the usual sealed canvas bag to be handed over to the government agent in Manaus. After that, I had two contract runs down-river for mining companies delivering mail and various bits and pieces.

It added up to a pretty full day and I arrived back at Manaus in the early evening with the intention of spending the night at the Palace and the prospect of a hot bath, a change of clothes, a decent meal, perhaps even a visit to *The Little Boat*, was more than attractive.

There wasn't much activity at the airstrip when I landed although on some days, you could find two or three planes parked by the hangars, in from down-river or the coast. There were still a couple of mechanics on duty and they helped me get the Bristol under cover for the night, then one of them gave me a lift into town in the company truck, an ancient Crossley tender.

When I entered the hotel, there was no sign of Juca behind the desk. In fact there was no one around at all so I went through the door on the left into the bar.

There seemed to be no one there either except for a rather romantic, or disreputable-looking figure, depending on your point of view, who stared at me from the full-length mirror at the other end.

I was badly in need of a shave and wore lace-up knee-length boots, whipcord breeches and leather flying jacket open to reveal the .45 automatic in its shoulder holster which

Hannah had insisted on giving me in place of the Webley, his theory being that there was no point in carrying a gun that wouldn't either stop a man dead in his tracks or knock him down.

I dropped my canvas grip to the floor, went behind the bar and helped myself to a bottle of cold beer from the ice-box. As I started to pour it into a glass, there was a slight, polite cough.

The woman who had come in through the open french windows from the terrace was a nun in tropical white, a small woman, not much over five feet in height with clear, untroubled eyes, not a wrinkle to be seen on that calm face in spite of her age which must have been fifty at least.

She spoke with the kind of accent that is associated with the New England States which made sense, for as I discovered later, she had been born and raised in the town of Vineyard Haven, Massachusetts, on the island of Martha's Vineyard.

'Mr Mallory?' she said.

'That's me.'

'We've been waiting for you. The *coman-dante* said you were expected back this evening. I am Sister Maria Teresa of the Little Sisters of Pity.'

She had said 'We'. I looked for another nun, but instead a young woman sauntered in from the terrace, a creature from another world than this, cool, elegant in a white chiffon frock, wide-brimmed straw hat, a blue silk scarf tied around it, the ends fluttering in the slight breeze. She carried an open parasol over one shoulder and stood, a hand on her hip, legs slightly apart, casually insolent as if challenging the world at large.

And there was one other peculiarity that made her herself alone – a silver bracelet about the right ankle, studded with tiny bells that jingled rather eerily as she walked, a sound that has haunted me for years. I couldn't see much of her face for with the evening sunlight behind her, the rest was in shadow.

Sister Maria Teresa said, 'This is Miss Joanna Martin. Her sister served with our mission at Santa Helena.'

I knew then, I suppose, what it was all

about, but played dumb. 'What can I do for you ladies?'

'We want to go up-river as soon as possible.'

'To Landro?'

'To start with, then Santa Helena.'

The simple directness of that remark was enough to take the breath away. I said, 'You've got to be joking.'

'Oh no, I assure you, Mr Mallory. I have complete authority from my *Order* to proceed to Santa Helena to assess the situation and to report on the feasibility of our carrying on there.'

'Carrying on?' I said stupidly.

She didn't appear to have heard me. 'And then there is the unfortunate business of Sister Anne Josepha and Sister Bernadette whose bodies were never recovered. I understand that in all probability they were taken alive by the Huna.'

'That would depend on your definition of living,' I said.

'You don't think it's possible?' It was the Martin girl who had spoken, the voice as cool and well-bred as you would have expected from the appearance, no strain there at all.

'Oh, it's possible.' I swallowed the impulse to give them the gory details on the kind of life captive women in such a situation could expect and contented myself by adding, 'Indians are very much like children and subject to sudden whims. One minute it seems like a good idea to carry off a couple of white women, the next, equally reasonable to beat them to death with an ironwood club.'

Sister Maria Teresa closed her eyes momentarily and Joanna Martin said in the same cool voice, 'But you can't be certain of that?'

'Any more than you can be that they're alive.'

'Sister Anne Josepha was Miss Martin's younger sister,' Maria Teresa said simply.

I'd suspected something like that, but it didn't make it any easier. I said, 'I'm sorry, but I know as much about Indians as most people and more than some. You asked me for my opinion and that's what I've given you.'

'Will you take us up to Landro with you

in the morning?' Sister Maria Teresa said. 'I understand from the *comandante* that we could fly from there to Santa Helena in under an hour.'

'Have you any idea what it's like up there?' I demanded. 'About as bad as any place on this earth could possibly be.'

'God will provide,' she said simply.

'He must have been taking a day off when the Huna took out Father Conté and the rest of them at Santa Helena,' I said brutally.

There was the briefest flash of pain on that calm face and then she smiled beautifully and with all the understanding in the world. 'The *comandante* told me you were one of those who found them. It must have been terrible for you.'

I said slowly, 'Look, Sister, the whole area comes under military jurisdiction.'

Joanna Martin came forward to join her, opened the embroidered handbag which hung from her wrist and took out a folded document which she tossed on the bar.

'Our authorisation to travel, counter-signed by the president himself.' Enough to bring

149

Alberto's heels together sharply, so much was certain and enough for me.

'All right, have it your own way. If you want to know what it's like to fly two hundred miles over some of the worst jungle in South America in the oldest plane in the territory, be at the airstrip at eight-thirty. As it happens, the rear cockpit's been enlarged to carry cargo, but there's only one seat. One of you will have to sit on the floor.'

I swallowed the rest of my beer and moved round the bar. 'And now you'll really have to excuse me. It's been a long day.'

Sister Maria Teresa nodded. 'Of course.'

Joanna Martin said nothing, simply picked up my grip and handed it to me, a gesture totally unexpected and quite out of character. My fingers touched hers as I took it and there was the perfume. God knows what it was but the effect was electrifying. I had never experienced such direct and immediate excitement from any woman and my stomach went hollow.

And she knew, damn her, I was certain of that, her mouth lifting slightly to one side as if in amusement at men and their perpetual hunger. I turned from that scorn and went out quickly.

There was still no sign of Juca but when I went up to my usual room, I found him turning down the sheets.

'Your bath is ready, Senhor Mallory,' he told me in that strange, melancholy whisper of his. 'You wish to eat here afterwards?'

I shook my head. 'I think I'll go out. If anyone wants me I'll be at *The Little Boat*.'

'The senhor has seen the ladies who were waiting for him downstairs?'

'Yes. Are they staying here?'

He nodded and withdrew and I stripped, pulled on an old robe and went along the corridor to the bathroom. The water was hot enough to bring sweat to my face and I lay there for half an hour, soaking away the fatigue of the day and thinking about the two women in the bar. Sister Maria Teresa was familiar enough. One of those odd people who live by faith alone and who seem to be able to survive most things, protected by the armour of their own innocence.

Joanna Martin's presence was more difficult to explain. God knows who had advised her to come. Certainly they must have an awful lot of pull between them to get hold of that authorisation with the president's signature on it. Colonel Alberto was not going to be pleased about that.

I went back to my room, towelling my head, briskly and started to dress. I'd actually got my trousers on and was pulling a clean linen shirt over my head when a slight noise made me turn quickly, one hand sliding towards the butt of the .45 automatic which lay on the dressing-table in its shoulder harness.

Joanna Martin moved in from the balcony, closing her parasol. 'Don't shoot,' she said coolly. 'I'm all I've got.'

I stood looking at her, without saying anything, noticing the face for the first time. Not really beautiful, yet different enough to make her noticeable in any crowd. Auburn hair, obviously regularly attended to by a top hairdresser. Good bones, an upturned nose that made her look younger than she was, hazel eyes spaced widely apart, curious golden flecks glinting in them.

I wondered how she'd look after a week up-river. I also wondered how that hair would look spread across a pillow. The physical ache was there again and disturbing in its intensity.

'The door was unlocked,' she explained. 'And the old man said you were in the bath. I thought I'd wait.'

I tucked in my shirt and reached for my shoulder harness. For some reason I found difficulty in speaking. That damned perfume, I suppose, the actual physical presence of her.

'Do you really need that thing?' she asked.

'It's a rough town after dark,' I said. 'Now what can I do for you?'

'Tell me the truth for a start.'

She moved back to the balcony. Outside the sky was orange and black, the sun a ball of fire. Standing there, against the light her legs were clearly outlined through the flimsy dress.

I said, 'I don't understand.'

'Oh, I think you do. You were being polite to Sister Maria Teresa down there in the bar. About my sister and the other girl, I mean. You were letting her down lightly.'

'Is that a fact?'

'Don't play games with me, Mr Mallory. I'm not a child. I want the truth.'

'Who in the hell do you think I am?' I demanded. 'The butler?'

I'm not sure why I got so angry – possibly because she'd spoken to me as if I were some sort of servant, but there was more to it than that. Probably some weird kind of defence mechanism to stop me from grabbing her.

'All right,' I said. 'I was asked if it was possible your sister and the other girl were still alive and I said it was. What else do you want to know?'

'Why would they take her? Why not kill her straight away. Even the older nuns were raped before being killed, isn't that so? I've read the report.'

'They like to freshen the blood,' I said. 'It's as simple as that.'

I started to turn away, tiring of it suddenly, wanting to be away from her, aware of the strain finally blowing through the surface.

She grabbed me by the shoulder and pulled me round. 'I want to know, damn you!' she cried. 'All of it.'

'All right,' I said and caught her wrists. 'It's a pretty complicated ritual. First of all, if they're virgins, they undergo a ceremonial defloration in front of everyone using a tribal totem. That's Huna custom with all maidens.'

There was horror in those eyes now and she had stopped struggling. 'Then for seven nights running, any warrior in the tribe is allowed to go in to them. It's a great honour. Any woman who doesn't become pregnant after that is stoned to death. Those outsiders who do are kept till the baby is born, then buried alive. The reasons for all this are pretty complicated, but if you have an hour to spare sometime I'll be happy to explain.'

She stared up at me, head moving from side to side and I added gravely, 'If I were you, Miss Martin, I'd pray she ended up in the river in the first place.'

The rage came up like hot lava and she pulled free of me, the left hand striking across my face and then the right, helpless, impotent anger and grief mingling together. She stumbled to the door, wrenched it open and ran into the corridor.

I walked to *The Little Boat*, a dangerous thing to do after dark, especially along the waterfront although such was the rage against life itself that filled me that I think it would have gone hard with any man who had crossed my path that night. I needed a drink and perhaps another to use one of Hannah's favourite phrases and a woman certainly – a dangerous mood to be in.

The Little Boat was not particularly busy, but that was only to be expected on a Monday night. The rumba band was playing, but there couldn't have been more than a dozen people on the floor. Lola, Hannah's girl friend from that first night was there, wearing the same red-satin dress. I rather liked her. She was an honest whore, but she was crazy about Hannah and made it obvious, her one weakness.

Knowing that he wouldn't be in that night she concentrated on me and she knew what she was about. Strange, but it didn't seem to work. I kept thinking of Joanna Martin and when I did that, Lola faded rapidly. The message got through to her after a while and she went off to try her luck elsewhere.

Which at least left me free to drink myself into a stupor if I was so inclined. I went up to that private section of the deck where I had dined with Hannah on that first night, ordered a meal and a bottle of wine to start with and closed the sliding doors.

My appetite seemed to have gone. I picked at my food, then went and stood at the rail, a bottle of wine in one hand and a glass in the other and stared out over the river. The reflected lights of the houseboats glowed in the water like candle flames. I was restless and ill at ease, waiting for something – wanting her, I suppose.

Behind me, the sliding doors opened, then closed again. I turned impatiently and found Joanna Martin standing there.

* * *

'Do you think we could start again?' she said.

There was a spare glass on the table. I filled it with wine and held it out to her. 'How did you find me?'

'Old Juca at the hotel. He was very kind. Got me a cab with a driver who bore a strong resemblance to King Kong. Gave him strict instructions to deliver me here in one piece.' She walked to the rail and looked out across the river. 'This is nice.'

I didn't know what to say, but she took care of it all more than adequately. 'I think we got off on the wrong foot. Mr Mallory. I'd like to try again.'

'Neil,' I said.

'All right.' She smiled. 'I'm afraid you've got the wrong impression of me entirely. Joanna Martin's my stage name. Originally I was just plain Joan Kowalski of Grantville, Pennsylvania.' Her voice changed completely, dropped into an accent she probably hadn't used in years. 'My daddy was a coalminer. What was yours?'

I laughed out loud. 'A small-town lawyer.

What we call a solicitor in England, at a place called Wells in Somerset. A lovely old town near the Mendip Hills.'

'It sounds marvellous.'

'It is, especially now in the autumn. Rooks in the elms by the cathedral. The dank, wet smell of rotting leaves blowing across the river.'

For a moment I was almost there. She leaned on the rail. 'Grantville was never like that. We had three things worth mentioning, none of which I ever wish to see again. Coalmines, steelworks and smoke. I didn't even look back once when I left.'

'And your sister?'

'We were orphaned when she was three and I was eight. The nuns raised me. I guess it became a habit with her.'

'And what about you?'

'I'm doing fine. Sing with some of the best bands in the country. Dorsey, Guy Lombardo, Sammy Kaye.' There was a perceptible change in her voice as she said this, a surface brashness as if she was really speaking for an audience. 'I've played second lead in two musicals in succession on Broadway.'

'All right,' I held up both hands defensively. 'I'm convinced.'

'And you?' She leaned back against the rail. 'What about you? Why Brazil?'

So I told her, from the beginning right up until that present moment, including a few items on the way that I don't think I'd ever mentioned to another living soul, such was the effect she had on me.

'So here we are,' she said at last when I was finished. 'The two of us at the edge of nowhere. It's beautiful, isn't it?'

The moon clouded over, sheet lightning flickered wildly, the rain came with a sudden rush bouncing from the awning above our heads.

'Romantic, isn't it?' I said. 'We get this every day of the week at sometime or another. Imagine what it's like in the rainy season.' I refilled her glass with wine. 'Bougainvilleas, acacias and God knows how many different varieties of poisonous snakes that can kill you in seconds. As for the river, if it isn't the alligators or *pirhanas*, it's water snakes so long they've been known to turn a canoe over and take the occupants down. Almost everything that looks nice is absolutely deadly. You should have tried Hollywood instead. Much safer on Stage 6.'

'That comes next month. I've got a screen test with M.G.M.' She smiled, then reached out to touch me, her hand flat against my chest, the smile fading. 'I've got to know, Neil. Just to know, one way or the other. Can you understand that?'

'Of course I can.' My hand fastened over hers and I was shaking like a kid on his first date. 'Would you like to dance?'

She nodded, moving against me and behind us, the sliding door was pulled open. 'So this is what you get up to when my back is turned?' Hannah said as he came through.

He was dressed in flying clothes and badly in need of a shave, but he was a romantic enough figure in his leather coat and breeches, a white scarf knotted carelessly about his neck.

He smiled with devastating charm and rushed forward with a sort of boyish eagerness, hands outstretched. 'And this will be Miss

Joanna Martin. Couldn't very well be anyone else.'

He held her hands in his for what seemed to me no good reason. I said, 'What in the hell is going on here?'

'You might as well ask, kid.' He yelled for the waiter and pulled off his coat. 'A lot happened since you left this morning. Alberto got through to me on the radio in the middle of the afternoon. Wanted me to pick him up at Santa Helena and fly him straight down to Manaus. We got in about an hour and a half ago. Met Miss Martin's companion at the hotel. When I left, she and the colonel were having quite an argument.'

'What's it all about?'

'That half-breed of Alberto's, the guy who'd lived with the Huna. Well, Alberto put him over the river last evening and by God, he was back at noon today.'

'You mean he'd made contact?'

'Sure had.' The waiter arrived at this point with a couple of bottles of Pouilly Fuisse in a bucket of water. 'According to him, all the tribesmen along the river had already heard what had happened to that village we visited and were scared stiff. A delegation of head men have agreed to meet Alberto a couple of miles up-river from the mission day after tomorrow.'

'Sounds too good to be true to me,' I said and meant it.

But Joanna Martin didn't think so. She sat down beside him and said eagerly, 'Do you think they'll be able to get news of my sister?'

'Certain to.' He took one of her hands again. 'It's going to be fine. I promise you.'

After that, to say that they got on like a house on fire would have been something of an understatement. I sat in the wings, as it were, and watched while they talked a lot, laughed a great deal and finally went down to join the small crowd on the dance floor.

I wasn't the only one who was put out. I caught a flash of scarlet in the half-light, Lola watching from behind a pillar. I knew then what the saying meant by a woman scorned. She looked capable of putting a knife between Hannah's shoulder blades if given half a chance.

I don't know what was said between the two on the floor, but when the band stopped playing, they moved across to the piano and Hannah sat down. As I've said before, he was a fair pianist and moved straight into a solid, pushing arrangement of *St Louis Blues* and Joanna Martin took the vocal.

She was good – better than I'd thought she would be. She gave it everything she had, a sort of total dedication and the crowd loved it. They followed with *Night and Day* and *Begin the Beguine* which was a tremendous hit that autumn and all one seemed to hear from radios everywhere, even on the River Amazon.

But by then I'd had enough. I left them to it, negotiated the catwalk to the jetty and walked morosely back to the hotel in the pouring rain.

I had been in bed for at least an hour, had just begun to drift into sleep when Hannah's voice brought me sharply to my senses. I got out of bed, padded to the door and opened it. He was obviously very drunk, standing with Joanna Martin outside the door of what I presumed must be her room at the end of the corridor.

He was trying to kiss her in that clumsy, unco-ordinated way a drunken man has. She obviously didn't need any assistance because she was laughing about it.

I closed the door, went back beneath the mosquito net and lit a cigarette. I don't know what I was shaking with – rage or thwarted desire, or both, but I lay there smoking furiously and cursing everyone who ever lived – until my door opened and closed again softly. The bolt clicked into place and there was silence.

I sensed her presence there in the darkness even before I smelled the perfume. She said, 'Stop sulking. I know you're in there. I can see your cigarette.'

'Bitch,' I said.

She pulled back the mosquito net, there was the rustle of some garment or other falling to the floor, then she slipped into bed beside me.

'That's nice,' she said and added, in the

same tone of voice, 'Colonel Alberto wants to be off at the crack of dawn. Sister Maria Teresa and I have strict instructions from Hannah to be at the airstrip not later than seven-thirty. He seems to think we'll be safer with him.'

'You suit yourself.'

'You're a good pilot, Neil Mallory, according to Hannah, the best he's ever known.' Her lips brushed my cheek. 'But you don't know much about women.'

I wasn't going to argue with her, not then, with the kind of need burning inside that could not be borne for long. As I pulled her to me, I felt the nipples blossom on her breasts, cool against my bare skin.

The excitement she aroused in me, the awareness, was quite extraordinary. But there was more to it than that. I lay there holding her, waiting for some sort of sign that might come or might not – the whole world waited. And in that timeless moment I knew, out of some strange foreknowledge, that whatever happened during the rest of my life, I'd never know anything better than this.

That whatever followed would always have the savour of anti-climax, just like Hannah.

She kissed me hard, mouth opening and the whole world came alive as lightning flickered across the sky and it started to rain again.

8

The Tree of Life

I awakened to sunlight streaming through the window, the mosquito net fluttering in the slight breeze. I was quite alone, at least as far as the bed went, but when I pushed myself up on one elbow I discovered Juca on the other side of the net placing a tray on the table.

'Breakfast, Senhor Mallory.'

'What time is it?'

He consulted a large, silver, pocket watch gravely. 'Eight o'clock exactly, senhor. The senhorita told me you wished to be awakened at this time.'

'I see – and when was this?'

'About an hour ago, senhor, when she was

leaving for the airstrip with the good Sister.
Will that be all, senhor?'

I nodded and he withdrew. I poured myself
a coffee and went to the window. They'd be
well on the way to Landro by now. Strange
the sense of personal loss and yet, in a way,
it was almost as if I was prepared for it. I
didn't feel like any breakfast after that, but
dressed quickly, had another cup of coffee
and went about my business.

There were several calls to make before
going out to the airstrip so I caught a cab in
front of the hotel. First of all there was the
mail, then some dynamo parts for one of the
mining agents at Landro and Figueiredo had
asked me to pick up a case of imported
London gin.

It was close to half past nine when I finally
arrived at the airstrip. A de Haviland Rapide
was parked by the tower and seemed to be
taking up all the ground staff's attention.
The Bristol was still under cover. I opened
the doors and the cab driver followed me in
with the crate of gin.

Joanna Martin was sitting in the pilot's

cockpit reading a book. She looked up and smiled brightly. 'What kept you?'

I couldn't think what to say for a moment, so great was my astonishment. I was only certain of one thing – that I had never been so pleased to see anyone. She knew it, I think, for the face softened for a moment.

'What happened?' I said.

'I decided to fly with you, that's all. I thought it would be more fun.'

'And what did Hannah have to say to that?'

'Oh, he wasn't too pleased.' She pushed herself up out of the cockpit, swung her legs over the edge and dropped into my arms. 'On the other hand, he did have rather a bad hangover.'

The cab driver had returned with the mail sack which he dropped on the ground beside the case of gin. He waited, mouth open in admiration and I paid him off and sent him on his way.

The moment we were alone, I kissed her and it was rather disappointing. Nothing like the night before, her lips cool and aseptic and she very definitely held me at arm's length.

She patted my cheek. 'Hadn't we better get moving?'

I couldn't think of anything that would explain the change although I suppose, on looking back on it all, I was guilty of simply expecting too much, still young enough to believe that if you loved someone they were certain to love you back.

Anyway, I loaded the freight behind the seat in the observer's cockpit and found her an old leather flying coat and helmet we kept for passengers. Three ground staff turned up about then, having seen us arrive and we got the Bristol outside.

I helped Joanna into the observer's cockpit and strapped her in. 'It's essential you keep your goggles on,' I warned. 'You'll find a hell of a lot of insects about, especially as we take off and land.'

When she pulled the goggles down, she seemed more remote than ever, another person altogether, but that was possibly just my imagination. I climbed into the cockpit, did my checks and wound the starting magneto, while the three mechanics formed a chain and pulled the propeller.

The engine broke into noisy life. I looked over my shoulder to check that she was all right. She didn't smile, simply nodded, so I eased the throttle open, taxied to the end of the runway, turned into the wind and took off feeling, for some unknown reason, thoroughly depressed.

The trip was something of a milk run for me by now, especially on a morning like this with perfect flying conditions. I suppose it must have had some interest for her although she certainly gave no sign of being particularly excited. In fact we only spoke twice over the voice pipe during the entire trip. Once as we turned up the Mortes from the Negro and I pointed out Forte Franco on the island below and again, as we approached Landor and I made preparations to land.

One thing did surprise me, the Hayley which was parked by the hangar. I had imagined it would be well on the way to Santa Helena by now.

As we rolled to a halt, Mannie came to meet us with a couple of labourers. He grinned up at me. 'What kept you? Sam's been like a cat on hot bricks, isn't that what you say?'

'I didn't know he cared,' I said and dropped to the ground.

'He doesn't,' he replied and elbowed me out of the way as I turned to help Joanna down. 'The privilege of age, Miss Martin.' He held up his hands.

She liked him, that much was obvious and her smile was of that special kind a woman reserves for a man she instantly recognises as good friend or father confessor. No strain, no cut-and-thrust, someone she would never have to surrender to or keep at arm's length.

I made some kind of lame, formal introduction. Mannie said, 'Now I understand why Sam's been acting as if he's been struck over the head with a Huna war club.' As I took off my flying helmet, he ruffled my hair. 'Has the boy here been treating you all right? Did he give you a good flight?'

I think it was the one and only time I ever felt angry with him and it showed for his smile faded slightly and there was concern in his eyes.

I turned away and Hannah came running across the airstrip rather fast considering the heat and the fact that he was dressed for flying. When he was about ten yards away, he slowed down as if suddenly realising he was making a fool of himself and came on at a walk.

He ignored me and said to Joanna Martin, 'Satisfied now?'

'Oh, I think you could say that,' she said coolly. 'Where's Sister Maria Teresa?'

'When I last saw her she was down at the jetty having a look at the mission launch. Had some sort of crazy idea that you and she might sleep on board.'

'What's wrong with the local hotel?'

'Just about everything so I've arranged for you both to move into my place. I'll take you up there now and show you round, then I've got to run Alberto up to Santa Helena.'

He picked up her suitcase and I said, 'What are the rest of us supposed to do?'

He barely glanced at me. 'We can manage in hammocks down here in the hangar for a few nights. Mannie's moved your gear out.'

He took her arm and they started to walk away. He paused after a few yards and called over his shoulder, 'I'd get that mail up to Figueiredo fast if I were you, kid. He's had the district runners standing by for an hour.'

'And that puts you in your place,' Mannie said and started to laugh.

For a moment, the anger flared up in me again and then, for some unaccountable reason, I found myself laughing with him. 'Women,' I said.

'Exactly. We have all the trees in the world and an abundance of fruit. All we needed was Eve.' He shook his head and picked up the mail sack. 'I'll take this up to Figueiredo for you. You go and have a cup of coffee and relax. I can see you've had a hard morning.'

He walked away towards town and I got my grip out of the Bristol and went into the hangar. He'd fixed three hammocks on the other side of the radio installation with a wall of packing cases five or six feet high to give some sort of privacy. There was a table and three chairs and a pot of coffee simmered gently on a double-ring oil stove.

I poured some into a tin mug, lit a cigarette and eased myself into one of the hammocks. I couldn't get Joanna Martin out of my mind – the change in her. It didn't seem to make any kind of sense at all, especially in view of the fact that she'd deliberately chosen to travel with me in the Bristol instead of in the Hayley.

My chain of thought was interrupted by Alberto who appeared in the gap in the end wall of packing cases. 'Camping out, I see, Mr Mallory.'

'Hannah isn't here. He took the Martin girl up to the house.'

'I am aware of that. It's you I want to see.' He found another tin mug and helped himself to coffee. 'I've spent most of the morning arguing with Sister Maria Teresa who insists on her right to proceed to Santa Helena.' He shook his head sadly. 'God protect me from the good and the innocent.'

'A formidable combination,' I said. 'Are you going to let her go?'

'I don't see how I can prevent it. 'You've seen the authorisation she and the Martin woman have? Counter-signed by the president himself.' He shrugged. 'If she decided to start up-river in the mission launch now, this very morning, how could I stop her, except by force and there would be the very devil to pay if I did that.'

'So what are you going to do?'

'You've heard my man managed to make contact with the Huna? Well, he's arranged a meeting for me tomorrow at noon in a patch of *campo* near the river about a mile upstream from the mission.'

'How many will be there?'

'One chief and five elders. It's a start, no more. A preliminary skirmish. I'm supposed to go on my own except for Pedro, of course, the half-breed who's made the contact for me. What do you think?'

'It should be quite an experience.'

'Yes, stimulating to put it mildly. I was wondering whether you might consider coming with me?'

The impudence of the request was

breathtaking. I sat up and swung my legs to the floor. 'Why me?'

'You know more about Indians than anyone else I know. You could be of considerable assistance in the negotiations.'

'How far is it to the river if we have to start running?'

He smiled. 'See how you feel about it tomorrow. Hannah will be flying the women in first thing in the morning. You could come with them. I've agreed to let them look over the mission.'

'Not that you had any choice in the matter.'

'Exactly.'

He moved out into the sunlight and Hannah came round the tail of the Hayley, buttoning the strap of his flying helmet, Mannie at his side.

'Okay, Colonel, let's go!' he called. 'The sooner I get you there, the sooner I'm back.'

'Can't you wait?' I asked.

He hesitated, the cabin door of the Hayley half-open, then turned very slowly. His face had a look on it I'd seen before that first night at *The Little Boat*, when he'd got rough with Lola.

He moved towards me and paused, no more than a foot in it. 'Just watch it, kid, that's all,' he said softly.

I told him what to do in good and concise Anglo-Saxon. I think for a moment there he was within an ace of having a go at me and then Mannie got between us, his face white. It wasn't really necessary for Hannah turned abruptly, climbed up into the cabin where Alberto was already waiting and shut the door. A moment later the engine burst into life and he taxied away.

He took off too fast, banking steeply across the river, barely making it over the trees, all good showy stuff and strictly for my benefit, just to make it clear who was boss.

Mannie said softly, 'This isn't good, Neil. Not good at all. You know what Sam can be like. How unpredictable he is.'

'You make all the allowances for him you want,' I said. 'But I'm damned if I will. Not any more.'

I left him there and walked along the edge of the airstrip towards the house. There was no sign of life when I got there, but the front door was open so I simply walked into the living-room.

I could hear the shower running so I lit a cigarette, sat on the window ledge and waited. After a while, the shower stopped. I could hear her singing and a little later, she entered the room dressed in an old robe, a towel tied around her head like a turban.

She stopped singing abruptly, eyebrows raised in surprise. 'And what can I do for you? Did you forget something?'

'You can tell me what I've done,' I said.

She stood there, looking at me calmly for a long, long moment, then moved to where her handbag lay on a bamboo table, opened it, found herself a cigarette and a small mother-of-pearl lighter.

She blew out in a long column of smoke and said calmly, 'Look, Mallory, I don't owe you a thing. All right?'

Even then I couldn't see it and in any case, after that, all I wanted to do was hurt her. I moved to the door and said, 'Just one thing. How much do I owe you?'

She laughed in my face and I turned, utterly

defeated, stumbled down the veranda steps and hurried away towards the river.

All right, so I didn't know much about women, but I hadn't deserved this. I wandered along the riverbank, a cigarette smouldering between my lips and finally found myself at the jetty.

There were several boats there, mainly canoes, but Figueiredo's official launch was tied up and another belonging to one of the big land company agents. The mission launch was at the far end, Sister Maria Teresa in the rear cockpit. I started to turn away, but it was already too late for she called to me by name and I had no choice, but to turn and walk down to the boat.

She smiled as I reached the rail. 'A beautiful morning, Mr Mallory.'

'For the moment.'

She nodded and said calmly, 'Would you have such a thing as a cigarette to spare?'

I was surprised and showed it I suppose as I produced a packet and offered her one. 'They're only local, I'm afraid. Black tobacco.'

She blew out smoke expertly and smiled. 'Don't you approve? Nuns are only human, you know, flesh and blood like anyone else.'

'I'm sure you are, Sister.' I started to turn away.

She said, 'I get the distinct impression that you do not approve of me, Mr Mallory. If I hadn't called out to you, you wouldn't have stopped to talk. Isn't that so?'

'All right,' I said. 'I think you're a silly, impractical woman who doesn't know what in the hell she's getting mixed up in.'

'I've spent seven years in South America as a medical missionary, Mr Mallory. Three of them in other parts of Northern Brazil. This kind of country is not entirely unfamiliar to me.'

'Which only makes it worse. Your own experience ought to tell you that by coming here at all, you've only made a tricky situation even more difficult for everyone who comes into contact with you.'

'Well, it's certainly a point of view,' she said good-humouredly. 'I've been told that you have a great deal of experience with

183

Indians. That you worked with Karl Buber on the Xingu.'

'I knew him.'

'A great and good man.'

'Who stopped being a missionary when he discovered you were doing the Indians as much harm as anyone else.'

She sighed. 'Yes, I would agree that the record has been far from perfect, even amongst the various religious organisations involved.'

'Far from perfect?' I was well into my stride now, my general anger and frustration at the morning's events finding a convenient channel. 'They don't need us, Sister, any of us. The best service we could offer them would be to go away and leave them alone and they certainly don't need your religion. They wear nothing worth speaking about, own nothing, wash themselves twice a day and help each other. Can your Christianity offer them more than that?'

'And kill each other,' she said. 'You forgot to mention that.'

'All right, so they look upon all outsiders as natural enemies. God alone knows, they're usually right.'

'They also kill the old,' she said. 'The disfigured, the mentally deficient. They kill for the sake of killing.'

I shook my head. 'No, you don't understand, do you? That's the really terrible thing. Death and life are one, part of existence itself in their terms. Waking, sleeping – it's all the same. How can it be bad to die, especially for a warrior? War is the purpose for which he lives.'

'I would take them love, Mr Mallory, is that such a bad thing?'

'What was it one of your greatest Jesuits said? The sword and the iron rod are the best kind of preaching.'

'A long, long time ago. As the times change so men change with them.' She stood up and straightened her belt. 'You accuse me of not really understanding and you may well have a point. Perhaps you could help me on the road to rehabilitation by showing me the sights of Landro.'

Defeated for the second time that morning, I resigned myself to my fate and took her hand to help her over the rail.

As we walked along the jetty, she took my arm and said, 'Colonel Alberto seems a very capable officer.'

'Oh, he's that, all right.'

'What is your opinion of this meeting he has arranged tomorrow with one of the Hun chieftains? Is it likely to accomplish much?'

'It all depends what they want to see him for,' I said. 'Indians are like small children – completely irrational. They can smile with you one minute and mean it – dash out your brains the next on the merest whim.'

'So this meeting could prove to be a dangerous undertaking?'

'You could say that. He's asked me to go with him.'

'Do you intend to?'

'I can't think of the slightest reason why I should at the moment, can you?'

She didn't get a chance to reply for at that moment her name was called and we looked up and found Joanna Martin approaching. She was dressed in the white chiffon dress again, wore the same straw hat and carried the parasol over one shoulder. She might have stepped straight off a page in Vogue and I don't think I've ever seen anything more incongruous.

Sister Maria Teresa said, 'Mr Mallory is taking me on a sight-seeing trip, my dear.'

'Well, that should take all of ten minutes.' Joanna Martin took her other arm, ignoring me completely.

We walked through the mean little streets with the hopeless faces peering out of the windows at us, the ragged half-starved children playing beneath the houses. An oxen had died in a side alley, obviously of some disease or other so that the flesh was not fit for human consumption. It had been left exactly where it had fallen and had swollen to twice its normal size. The smell was so terrible that it even managed to kill the stink from the cesspool a few yards farther on which had over-flowed and ran in a steady stream down the centre of the street.

She didn't like any of it, nor for that matter did Joanna Martin. I pointed out the steam house, one of those peculiarities of up-river villages where Indians went through regular purification for religious reasons with the help of red-hot stones and lots of cold water, but it didn't help.

We moved out through a couple of streets of shanties constructed of iron and pieces of packing cases and inhabited mainly by forest Indians who had made the mistake of trying to come to terms with the white man's world.

'Strange,' I said, 'but in the forest, naked as the day they were born, most of these women look beautiful. Put them in a dress and something inexplicable happens. Beauty goes, pride goes . . .'

Joanna Martin put a hand out to stay me. 'What was that, for God's sake?'

We were past the final line of huts, close to the river and the edge of the jungle. The sound came again, a sharp bitter cry. I led the way forward, then paused.

On the edge of the trees by the river, an Indian woman knelt in front of a tree, arms raised above her head, a tattered calico dress pulled up above her thighs. The man with her was also Indian in spite of his cotton trousers and shirt. He was tying her wrists above her head by lianas to a convenient branch.

The woman cried out again, Sister Maria Teresa took a quick step forward and I pulled her back. 'Whatever happens, you mustn't interfere.'

She turned to me and said, 'This is one custom with which I am entirely familiar, Mr Mallory. I will stay here for a while if you don't mind. I may be able to help afterwards, if she'll let me.' She smiled. 'Amongst other things, I'm a qualified doctor, you see. If you could bring me my bag along from the house at some time, I'd be most grateful.

She went towards the woman and her husband and sat down on the ground a yard or two away. They completely ignored her.

Joanna Martin gripped my arm fiercely. 'What is it?'

'She's going to have a child,' I said. 'She's tied by her wrists with lianas so that the child is born while she is upright. That way he will be stronger and braver than a child born to a woman lying down.'

The woman gave another low moan of

pain, her husband squatted on the ground beside her.

Joanna Martin said, 'But this is ridiculous. They could be here all night.'

'Exactly,' I said. 'And if Sister Maria Teresa insists on behaving like Florence Nightingale, the least we can do is go back to the house and get that bag for her.'

On the way back through Landro, a rather unusual incident took place which gave me a glimpse of another side of her character.

As we came abreast of a dilapidated house on the corner of a narrow street, a young Indian girl of perhaps sixteen or seventeen rushed out of the entrance on to the veranda. She wore an old calico dress and was barefoot, obviously frightened to death. She glanced around her hurriedly as if debating which way to run, started down the steps, missed her footing and went sprawling. A moment later Avila rushed out of the house, a whip in one hand. He came down the steps on the run and started to belabour her.

I didn't care for Avila and certainly didn't

like what he was doing to the girl, but I'd learned to move cautiously in such cases for this was still a country where most women took the occasional beating as a matter of course.

Joanna Martin was not so prudent, however. She went in like a battleship under full sail and lashed out at him with her handbag. He backed away, a look of bewilderment on his face. I got there as quickly as I could and grabbed her arm as she was about to strike him again.

'What's she done?' I asked Avila and pulled the girl up from the ground.

'She's been selling herself round the town while I've been away,' he said. 'God knows what she might have picked up.'

'She's yours?'

He nodded. 'A Huna girl. I bought her just over a year ago.'

We'd spoken in Portuguese and I turned to give Joanna a translation. 'There's nothing to be done. The girl belongs to him.'

'What do you mean, belongs to him?'

'He bought her, probably when her parents

died. It's common enough up-river and legal.'

'Bought her?' First there was incredulity in her eyes, then a kind of white-hot rage. 'Well, I'm damn well buying her back,' she said. 'How much will this big ape take?'

'Actually he speaks excellent English,' I said. 'Why not ask him yourself.'

She was really angry by then, scrabbled in her handbag and produced a hundred *cruzeiro*, note which she thrust at Avila. 'Will this do?'

He accepted it with alacrity and bowed politely. 'A pleasure to do business with you, senhorita,' he said and made off rapidly up the street in the direction of the hotel.

The girl waited quietly for whatever new blow fate had in store for her, that impassive Indian face giving nothing away. I questioned her in Portuguese which she seemed to understand reasonably well.

I said to Joanna. 'She's a Huna all right. Her name is Christina and she's sixteen. Her father was a wild rubber tapper. He and the mother died from smallpox three years ago. Some woman took her in then sold her to

Avila last year. What do you intend to do with her?'

'God knows,' she said. 'A shower wouldn't be a bad idea to start with, but it's more Sister Maria Teresa's department than mine. How much did I pay for her, by the way?'

'About fifty dollars – a hundred *cruzeiros*. Avila can take his pick of girls like her for ten which leaves him ninety for booze.'

'My God, what a country,' she said, and taking Christina by the hand, started down the street towards the airstrip.

I spent the afternoon helping Mannie do an engine check on the Bristol. Hannah arrived back just after six and was in excellent spirits. I lay in my hammock and watched him shave while Mannie prepared the evening meal.

Hannah was humming gaily to himself and looked years younger. When Mannie asked him if he wanted anything to eat he shook his head and pulled on a clean shirt.

I said, 'You're wasting your time, Mannie. His appetite runs to other things tonight.'

Hannah grinned. 'Why don't you give in,

kid? I mean that's a real woman. She's been there and back and that kind need a man.'

He turned his back and went off whistling as I swung my legs to the floor. Mannie grabbed me by the arm. 'Let it go, Neil.'

I stood up, walked to the edge of the hangar and leaned against a post looking out over the river, taking time to calm down. Funny how easily I got worked up over Hannah these days.

Mannie appeared and pushed a cigarette at me. 'You know, Neil, women are funny creatures. Not at all as we imagine them. The biggest mistake we make is to see them as we think they should be. Sometimes the reality is quite different . . .'

'All right, Mannie, point taken.' Great heavy spots of rain darkened the dry earth and I took down an oilskin coat and pulled it on. 'I'll go and check on Sister Maria Teresa. I'll see you later.'

I'd taken up her bag of tricks, an oilskin coat and a pressure lamp, earlier in case the vigil proved to be a prolonged one. Just as I reached the outer edge of Landro, I met her on the way in with the mother walking beside her carrying her newly-born infant in a blanket, the father following behind.

'A little girl,' Sister Maria Teresa announced, 'but they don't seem to mind. I'm going to stay the night with them. Will you let Joanna know for me?'

I accompanied them through the gathering darkness to the shack the couple called home, then I went back along the street to the hotel.

The rain was really coming down now in great solid waves and I sat at the bar with Figueiredo for a while, playing draughts and drinking some of that gin I'd brought in for him, waiting for it to stop.

After an hour, I gave up, lit my lamp and plunged down the steps into the rain. The force was really tremendous. It was like being in a small enclosed world, completely alone and for some reason, I felt exhilarated.

Light streamed through the closed shutters when I went up the steps to the veranda of the house and a gramophone was playing. I stood there for a moment listening to the murmur of voices, the laughter, then knocked on the door.

Hannah opened it. He was in his shirtsleeves

and held a glass of Scotch in one hand. I didn't give him a chance to say anything.

I said, 'Sister Maria Teresa's spending the night in Landro with a woman who's just had a baby. She wanted Joanna to know.'

He said, 'Okay, I'll tell her.'

As I turned away Joanna appeared behind him, obviously to see what was going on. It was enough. I said, 'Oh, by the way, I'll be flying up to Santa Helena with you in the morning. The mail run will have to wait.'

His face altered, became instantly wary. 'Who says so?'

'Colonel Alberto. Wants me to take a little walk with him tomorrow to meet some Huna. I'll be seeing you.'

I went down into the rain. I think she called my name, though I could not be sure, but when I glanced back over my shoulder, Hannah had moved out on to the veranda and was looking after me.

Some kind of small triumph, I suppose, but one that I suspected I would have to pay dearly for.

9

Drumbeat

I did not sleep particularly well and the fact that it was three a.m. before Hannah appeared didn't help. I slept only fitfully after that and finally got up at six and went outside.

It was warm and oppressive, unusually so considering the hour, and the heavy grey clouds promised rain of the sort that would last for most of the day. Not my kind of morning at all and the prospect of what was to follow had little to commend it.

I wandered along the front of the open hangar and paused beside the Bristol which stood there with its usual air of expectancy as if waiting for something to happen. It came to me suddenly that other men must have stood beside her like this, coughing over the first cigarette of the day as they waited to go out on a dawn patrol, sizing up the weather, waiting to see what the day would bring. It gave me a curious feeling of kinship which didn't really make any sense.

I turned and found Hannah watching me. That first time we'd met after I'd crash-landed in the Vega, I'd been struck by the ageless quality in his face, but not now. Perhaps it was the morning or more probably the drink from the previous night, but he looked about a hundred years old. As if he had experienced everything there ever was and no longer had much faith in what was to come.

The tension between us was almost tangible. He said harshly, 'Do you intend to go through with this crazy business?'

'I said so, didn't I?'

He exploded angrily. 'God damn it, there's no knowing how the Huna might react. If they turn sour, you won't have a prayer.'

'I can't say I ever had much faith in it anyway.' I started to move past him.

He grabbed my arm and spun me round.

'What in the hell are you trying to prove, Mallory?'

I see now, on reflection, that he saw the whole thing as some sort of personal challenge. If I went, then he would have to go or appear less than me and not only to Joanna Martin, for as I have said, he was a man to whom appearances were everything.

He was angry because I had put him in an impossible position which should have pleased me. Instead I felt as sombre as that grey morning itself.

'Let's just say I'm tired of life and leave it at that.'

And for a moment, he believed me enough to slacken his grip so that I was able to pull free. As I walked back along the edge of the hangar, the first heavy drops of rain pattered against the roof.

The run to Santa Helena was uneventful enough in spite of the bad weather. We didn't get away until much later than had been anticipated because of poor visibility, but from nine o'clock on, there was a perceptible lightening in the sky although the rain still fell heavily and Hannah decided to chance it.

He asked me to take the controls which suited me in the circumstances for it not only kept me out of Joanna Martin's way, but also meant that I didn't have to struggle to find the right things to say to Sister Maria Teresa. I left all that to Hannah who seemed to do well enough although for most of the time the conversation behind was unintelligible to me, bound up as I was in my thoughts.

The situation at Santa Helena was no better. The same heavy rain drifting up from the forest again in grey mist because of the heat, but landing was safe enough and I put the Hayley down with hardly a bump.

I had radioed ahead on take-off and had given them an estimated time of arrival. In spite of this I was surprised to find Alberto himself waiting to greet us with the guard detail at the side of the strip.

He came forward to meet us as the Hayley rolled to a halt and personally handed the two women down from the cabin, greeting them courteously. His face beneath the peaked officer's cap was serious and he presented a melancholy figure, adrift in an alien landscape. The caped cavalry greatcoat he wore was obviously an echo of better days.

He led the way back to the small jetty where the motor launch waited. It presented a formidable appearance. There was a Lewis gun on the roof of the main saloon, another in the prow, each protected by sandbags, and a canvas screen along each side of the boat deck made it possible to move unobserved and also provided some sort of cover against arrows.

An awning had been rigged in the stern against the rain, there was a cane table and canvas chairs and as we approached, an orderly came out of the saloon carrying a tray. He wore white gloves and as the ladies seated themselves, served coffee from a silver pot in delicate china cups. The rain hammered down, a couple of alligators drifted by. A strange, mad dream standing there by the rail with only the stench of rotting vegetation rising from the river to give it reality.

Alberto approached and offered me a

cigarette. 'In regard to our conversation yesterday, Senhor Mallory. Have you come to any decision?'

'A hell of a morning for a walk in the forest,' I said, peering out under the awning. 'On the other hand, it could be interesting.'

He smiled slightly, hesitated, as if about to say something, obviously thought better of it and turned away leaving me at the rail on my own. To say that I instantly regretted my words was certainly not so and yet I had voluntarily committed myself to a situation of grave danger which made no kind of sense at all. Now why was that?

A couple of soldiers were already casting-off and the launch eased away from the jetty. Alberto accepted a cup of coffee from the orderly and said, 'There won't be time to drop you at Santa Helena at the moment. The Huna have changed our meeting-place to the site of an older rubber plantation, a ruined *fazenda* about five miles up-river from here and a mile inland. The appointed hour is still the same however, noon, so we shall barely make the rendezvous on time as it is.

Under the circumstances, I'm afraid you'll all have to come along for the ride.'

'May I ask what your plans are, Colonel?' Sister Maria Teresa inquired.

'Simplicity itself, Sister.' He smiled wearily. 'I go to talk peace with the Huna as my superiors, who are at present sitting on their backsides a good thousand miles from here behind their desks, insist.'

'You don't approve?'

'Let us say I am less than sanguine as to the result. A delegation, one chief and five elders, has agreed to meet me on their terms which means I go alone, except for my interpreter and very definitely unarmed. The one change in the arrangement so far is that Senhor Mallory, who knows more about Indians than any man I know, has agreed to accompany me.'

Joanna Martin went very still, her coffee cup raised halfway to her mouth. She turned and looked at me fixedly, a slight frown on her face.

Sister Maria Teresa said, 'A long walk, Mr Mallory.'

Hannah was good and angry, glared at me, eyes wild, then at Joanna Martin. He didn't like what he was going to say but he got it out, I'll say that for him. 'You can count me in too, Colonel.'

'Don't be stupid,' I cut in. 'Who in the hell would be left to fly the women out in the Hayley if anything went wrong?'

There was no arguing with that and he knew it. He turned away angrily and Sister Maria Teresa said, 'It has been my experience in the past, Colonel, that Indians do not look upon any group containing a woman as a threat to them. Wouldn't you agree, Mr Mallory?'

Alberta glanced quickly at me, aware instantly, as I was myself, of what was in her mind. I said, 'Yes, that's true up to a point. They certainly don't take women to war themselves, but I wouldn't count on it.'

'A risk I am prepared to take,' she said simply.

There was a short silence. Alberto shook his head. 'An impossibility, Sister. You must see that.'

There are times when the naîveté of the truly good can be wholly infuriating. She said, with that disarming smile of hers, 'I am as much for peace as you, Colonel, but I also have a special interest here, remember. The fate of Sister Anne Josepha and her friend.'

'I would have thought the church had martyrs in plenty, Sister,' he replied.

Joanna Martin stood up. 'That sounds to me like another way of saying you don't really expect to come back. Am I right?'

'*Se Deusquiser*, senhorita.'

If God wills. Joanna Martin turned to me, white faced. 'You must be mad. What are you trying to prove?'

'You want to know if your sister's alive, don't you?' I asked.

She went into the saloon, banging the door behind her. Sister Maria Teresa said patiently, 'Am I to take it that you refuse to allow me to accompany you, Colonel?'

'Under no circumstances, Sister.' He saluted her gravely. 'A thousand regrets, but I am in command here and must do as I see fit.'

'In spite of my authorisation?'

'Sister, the Pope himself could not make me take you with us today.'

I think it was only then that she really and truly appreciated the danger of the entire undertaking. She sighed heavily. 'I did not understand before. I think I do now. You are brave men, both of you.'

'I do my duty only, Sister,' he said, 'but I thank you.'

She turned to me. 'Duty in your case also, Mr Mallory?'

'You know what they say, Sister.' I shrugged. 'I go because it's there.'

But there were darker reasons than that – I knew it and so did she for it showed in her eyes. I thought she might say something – a personal word, perhaps. Instead she turned and followed Joanna into the saloon.

Hannah threw his cigarette over the rail in a violent gesture. 'You're dead men walking. A dozen arrows apiece waiting for each of you up there.'

'Perhaps.' Alberto turned to me. 'The stipulation is that we go unarmed. What do you think?'

'As good a way of committing suicide as any?'

'You don't trust them?'

'Can you trust the wind?' I shook my head. 'As I've said before, whatever they do will be entirely as the mood takes them. If they decide to kill us instead of talking, it won't be out of any conscious malice, but simply because it suddenly strikes them as a better idea than the last one they had.'

'I see. Tell me, what was Karl Buber's attitude regarding guns?'

'He was never without one prominently displayed, if that's what you mean. Forest Indians fear guns more than anything else I can think of. It doesn't mean they won't attack you if you're armed, but they'll think twice. They still think it's some sort of big magic.'

'And yet they demand that we go unarmed.' He sighed. 'An unhealthy sign, I'm afraid.'

'I agree. On the other hand, what the eye doesn't see . . .'

'The same thought had occurred to me, I must confess. That oilskin coat of yours, for example, is certainly large enough to conceal a multitude of sins.'

He was suddenly considerably more cheerful at the prospect, I suppose, of finding himself with a fighting chance again.

'I'll see to the necessary preparations,' he said. 'We'll go over things in detail closer to the time.'

He went along the deck to the wheelhouse leaving me alone with Hannah. His face was white, eyes glaring. For a moment I thought he might take a punch at me. He didn't get the chance because Joanna chose that precise moment to appear from the saloon.

I could have sworn from her eyes that she had been crying, although that didn't seem possible, but there was fresh powder on her face and the wide mouth had been smeared with vivid orange lipstick.

She spoke to Hannah without looking at him. 'Would you kindly get to hell out of here, Sam? I'd like a private word with Galahad here.'

Hannah glanced first at her, then at me and went without argument, some indication of the measure of control she had over him by then, I suppose.

She moved in close enough to make her presence felt. 'Are you doing this for me?'

'Not really,' I said. 'I just like having a good time.'

She slapped me across the face hard enough to turn my head sideways. 'Damn you, Mallory,' she cried. 'I don't owe you a thing.'

She did the last thing I would have expected. Flung her arm about my neck and fastened that wide mouth of hers on mine. Her body moved convulsively and for a moment it was difficult to consider other things. And then she pulled free of me, turned and ran into the saloon.

None of it made a great deal of sense, but then human actions seldom do. I moved along the starboard rail to the prow and paused to light a cigarette beside the Lewis gun which was for the moment unmanned in its sand-bagged emplacement.

There was a stack of 47-round drum magazines ready for action at the side of the trim, deadly-looking gun and I sat down on the sandbags to examine it.

'The first gun ever fired from an aeroplane.' Hannah appeared from the other side of the wheelhouse. 'That was June 7, 1912. Shows how long they've been around.'

'Still a lot around back home,' I said. 'We used them in Wapitis.'

He nodded. 'The Belgian Rattlesnake the Germans called it during the war. The best light aerial gun we had.'

There was silence. Rain hissed into the river, ran from the brim of my wide straw sombrero. I couldn't think of a thing to say, didn't even know what he wanted. And even then, he surprised me by saying exactly the opposite of what I had expected.

'Look, kid, let's get it straight. She's my kind of woman. You saw her first, but I was there last and that's what counts, so hands off, understand?'

Which at least meant he expected me to survive the day's events and unaccountably cheered, I smiled in his face. Poor Sam. For a moment I thought again he might hit me. Instead he turned wildly and rushed away.

* * *

The place was marked on the large-scale map for the area as Matamoros and we found it with no trouble at all. There was an old wooden jetty rotting into the river and a landing stage almost overgrown, but the track to the house, originally built wide enough to take a cart, was still plain.

We moved into the landing stage, a couple of men ready at each Lewis gun, another ten behind the canvas screen on the starboard side, rifles ready, my old comrade-in-arms Sergeant Lima in charge.

We bumped against the landing stage not twenty yards away from that green wall and a couple of men went over the rail and held her in on hand-lines, the engine gently ticking over, ready to take us out of trouble with a burst of power if necessary.

But nothing happened. A couple of alligators slid off a mud-bank, a group of howler monkeys shouted angrily from the trees. The rest was silence.

Alberto said, 'Good, now we make ready.'

We went into the saloon where Joanna, Sister Maria Teresa and Hannah sat at the table talking in low voices. They stopped as we entered, Alberto, Pedro the half-breed interpreter and myself, and stood up.

I took off my yellow oilsin coat and Alberto opened the arms cupboard and produced a Thompson sub-machine-gun with a drum magazine which we'd prepared earlier with a specially lengthened sling. I slipped it over my right shoulder, muzzle down and Hannah helped me on with my coat again.

Alberto took a gun which was, I understood, his personal property – probably one of the most deadly hand-guns ever made: the Model 1932 Mauser machine-pistol, and he gave Pedro a .45 automatic to stick in his waistband under the ragged poncho he wore.

The interpreter was something of a surprise for I had expected at least some sign of his white blood and found none. He looked all Huna to me in spite of his white man's clothing.

To finish, Alberto produced a couple of Mills grenades, slipped one in his pocket and handed the other to me. 'Another little extra.' He smiled lightly. 'Just in case.'

There was some confused shouting outside. As we turned, the saloon door was flung open and Sergeant Lima stood there, mouth gaping.

'What is it, man?' Alberto demanded and Hannah produced the .45 automatic from his shoulder holster with a speed which could only indicate considerable practice.

'The holy Sister, Colonel,' Lima croaked. 'She has gone into the jungle.'

There was dead silence and Joanna Martin slumped into a chair and started to whisper a Hail Mary, probably for the first time in years.

Alberto said savagely, 'Good God, man, how could such a thing be? You were supposed to be guarding the deck. You were in command.'

'As God is my witness, Colonel.' Lima was obviously terrified. 'One second she was standing there, the next, she was over the rail and into the jungle before we realised what was happening.'

Which was too much, even for the kind of rigidly correct professional soldier that Alberto was. He slapped him backhanded across the face, threw him into a chair and turned to Hannah.

'Captain Hannah, you will oblige me by taking charge here. I suggest you keep the launch in midstream till our return. If this miserable specimen gives you even a hint of trouble, shoot him.' He turned to me. 'And now, my friend, I think we move very fast indeed.'

Pedro was first over the rail and Alberto and I were not far behind. The launch was already moving out into the current as we reached the edge of the forest. I glanced back over my shoulder, caught a glimpse of Hannah standing in the stern under the awning, a machine-gun in his hands, Joanna Martin at his shoulder. God knows why, but I waved, some sort of final gallant gesture, I suppose, then turned and plunged into that green darkness after Alberto.

As I have said, the track had been built wide enough to accommodate reasonably heavy traffic and I now discovered that it had exceptionally solid foundations, logs of ironwood, embedded into the soft earth for its entire length. The jungle had already moved in on it to a considerable extent, but it still gave a quick, clear passage through the kind of country that would have been about as penetrable as a thorn thicket to a white man.

The branches above were so thickly intertwined that virtually no rain got through and precious little light either. The gloom was quite extraordinary and rather eerie.

Pedro was well ahead, running very fast and soon disappeared from sight. I followed hard on Alberto's heels. After a while, we heard a cry and a few yards farther on found Pedro and Sister Maria Teresa standing together.

Alberto kept his temper remarkably under the circumstance. He simply said, 'This is foolishness of the worst kind, Sister. I must insist that you return with us at once.'

'And I, Colonel, am as equally determined to carry on,' she said.

I was aware of the forest foxes calling to each other in the jungle on either side and knew that it was already too late to go back, perhaps for all of us. The thing I was most conscious of was my contempt for her stupidity, a feeling not so much of anger, but of frustration at her and so many like her who out of their own pig-headed insistence on doing good ended up causing more harm than a dozen Avilas.

There was some sort of thud in the shadows a yard or two behind. My hand went through the slit in my pocket and found the grip and trigger guard of the Thompson. There was a Huna lance embedded in the earth beside the track, a necklace of monkey skulls hanging from it.

'What does it mean?' Sister Maria Teresa asked.

'That we are forbidden to go back,' Alberto said. 'The decision as to what to do with you is no longer mine to make, Sister. If it is of any consolation to you at all, you have probably killed us all.'

At the same moment, a drum started to boom hollowly in the middle distance.

We put a bold face on it, the only thing to do and moved on, Pedro in the lead, Sister

Maria Teresa following. Alberto and I walked shoulder-to-shoulder at the rear.

We were not alone for the forest was alive with more than wild life. Birds coloured in every shade of the rainbow lifted out of the trees in alarm and not only at our passing. Parrots and macaws called angrily to each other.

'What did you say?' I murmured to Alberto. 'A chief and five elders?'

'Don't rub it in,' he said. 'I've a feeling this is going to get considerably worse before it gets better.'

The drum was louder now and somehow the fact that it echoed alone made it even more sinister. There was the scent of wood-smoke on the damp air and then the trees started to thin and suddenly it was lighter and then the gable of a house showed clear and then another.

Not that it surprised me for in the great days of the Brazilian rubber boom, so many millions were being made that some of the houses on the plantations up-country were small palaces, with owners so wealthy they could afford to pay private armies to defend them against the Indians. But not now. Those days were gone and Matamoros and places like it crumbled into the jungle a little bit more each year.

We emerged into a wide clearing, what was left of the house on the far side. The drumming stopped abruptly. Our hosts were waiting for us in the centre.

The *cacique* or chief was easily picked out and not only because he was seated on a log and had by far the most magnificent head-dress, a great spray of macaw feathers. He also sported a wooden disc in his lower lip which pushed it a good two inches out from his face, a sign of great honour amongst the Huna.

His friends were similarly dressed. Beautifully coloured feather head-dresses, a six-foot bow, a bark pouch of arrows, a spear in the right hand. Their only clothing, if that's what you could call it, was a bark penis sheath and various necklaces and similar ornaments of shells, stones or human bone.

The most alarming fact of all was that they were all painted for war, the entire skin surface being coated with an ochre-coloured mud peculiar to that section of the river. They were angry and showed it, hopping from one foot to the other, rattling on at each other like a bunch of old women in the curiously sibilant whispering that passed for speech amongst them and the anger on their flat, sullen faces was as the rage of children and as unpredictable in its consequences.

The chief let loose a broadside. Pedro said, 'He wants to know why the holy lady and Senhor Mallory are here? He's very worried. I'm not sure why.'

'Maybe he intended to have us killed out of hand,' I said to Alberto, 'and her presence has thrown him off balance.'

He nodded and said to Pedro, 'Translate as I speak. Tell him the Huna have killed for long enough. It is time for peace.'

Which provoked another outburst, the general gist of which was that the white men had started it in the first place which entitled the Huna to finish. If all the white men went from the Huna lands, then things might be better.

Naturally Alberto couldn't make promises of that kind and in any case, he was committed to a pretty attacking form of argument. The Huna had raided the mission at Santa Helena, had murdered Father Conté and many nuns.

The chief tried to deny this although he didn't stand much of a chance of being believed with a nun's rosary and crucifix hanging around his neck. His elders shuffled from foot to foot again, scowling like schoolboys in front of the head-master so Alberto piled on the pressure. They had already seen what the government could do. Did they wish the white man's great bird to drop more fire from the sky on their villages?

One by one, more Indians had been emerging from the forest into the clearing. I had been aware of this for some time and so had Alberto, but he made no reference to it. They pressed closer, hanging together in small groups, shouting angrily. I won't say working up their courage for fear didn't enter their thinking.

I glanced once at Sister Maria Teresa and found her – how can I explain it? – transfixed, hands clasped as if in prayer, eyes shining with compassion, presumably for these brands to be plucked from the flames.

It was round about then that Alberto raised the question of the two missing nuns. The response was almost ludicrous in its simplicity. From denying any part in the attack on Santa Helena in the first place, the chief now just as vehemently denied taking any female captives. All had been killed except for those who had got away.

Which was when Alberto told him he was lying because no one had got away. The chief jumped up for the first time and loosed off another broadside, stabbing his finger repeatedly at Pedro. I noticed the outsiders had crept in closer now in a wide ring which effectively cut off our retreat to the forest.

Alberto gave me a cigarette and lit one himself nonchalantly. 'It gets worse by the minute. He called me here to kill me, I am certain of that now. How many do you make it out there?'

'At least fifty.'

'I may have to kill someone to encourage the others. Will you back me?'

Before I could reply, the chief shouted again.

Pedro said, 'He's getting at me now. He says I've betrayed my people.'

In the same moment an arrow hissed through the rain and buried itself in his right thigh. He dropped to one knee with a cry and two of the elders raised their spears to throw, howling in unison.

I had already unbuttoned the front of my oilskin coat in readiness for something like this, but I was too slow. Alberto drew and fired the Mauser very fast, shooting them both in the body two or three times, the heavy bullets lifting them off their feet.

The rest turned and ran and I loosed off a quick burst to send them on their way, deliberately aiming to one side, ripping up the earth in fountains of dirt and stone.

Within seconds there was not an Indian to be seen. Their voices rose angrily from the jungle all the way round the clearing. When I turned, Pedro was on his feet, Sister Maria Teresa crouched beside him tugging at the arrow. 'You're wasting your time, Sister,' I told her. 'Those things are barbed. He'll need surgery to get the arrowhead out.'

'He's right,' Pedro said, and reached down and snapped off the shaft as close to his thigh as possible.

'Right, let's get moving,' Alberto said. 'And be prepared to pick up your skirts and run if you want to live, Sister.'

'A moment, please, Colonel.'

One of the two men he had shot was already dead, but the other was having a hard time of it, blood bubbling between his lips with each breath. To my astonishment she knelt beside him, folded her hands and began to recite the prayers for the dying.

'Go Christian soul from this world, in the name of God the Father Almighty who created thee . . .'

Her voice moved on, Alberto shrugged helplessly and removed his cap. I followed suit with some reluctance, aware of the shrill cries of rage from the forest, thinking of that half-mile of green tunnel to the jetty. It suddenly came to me, with a sense of surprise, that I was very probably going to die.

Amazing what a difference that made. I was aware of the rain, warm and heavy, the blood on the dying man's mouth. No colour had ever seemed richer. The green of the trees, the heavy scent of wood-smoke from somewhere near at hand.

Was there much to regret? Not really. I had done what I wanted to do against all advice and every odds possible and it had been worth it. I could have been a junior partner in my father's law firm now and safe at home, but I had chosen to go to the margin of things. Well, so be it . . .

The Huna's final breath eased out in a dying fall, Sister Maria Teresa finished her prayers, stood up and turned her shining face towards us.

'I am ready now, gentlemen.'

I was no longer angry. There was no point. I simply took her arm and pushed her after Alberto who had turned and started towards the beginning of the track, Pedro limping beside him.

As we approached the forest I half expected a hail of arrows, but nothing came. Pedro said, 'They will wait for us on the track, Colonel. Play with us for a while. It is their way.'

Alberto paused and turned to me. 'You agree with him?'

I nodded. 'They like their fun. It's a game to them, remember. They'll probably try to frighten us to death for most of the way and actually strike when we think we are safe, close to the river.'

'I see. So the main thing to remember is to walk for most of the way and run like hell over the last section?'

'Exactly.'

He turned to Sister Maria Teresa. 'You heard, Sister?'

'We are in God's hands,' she said with that saintly smile of hers.

'And God helps those who help themselves,' Alberto told her.

A group of Indians had filtered out of the forest perhaps fifty yards to the right. He took his Mills bomb from his pocket, pulled the pin and threw it towards them. They were hopelessly out of range, but the explosion had a more than salutary effect. They vanished into the forest and all voices were stilled.

225

'By God, I may have stumbled on something,' he said. 'Let them sample yours also, my friend.'

I tossed it into the middle of the clearing, there was a satisfactorily loud explosion, birds lifted angrily out of the trees, but not one single human voice was to be heard.

'You like to pray, Sister?' Alberto said, taking her by the arm. 'Well, pray that silence lasts us to the jetty.'

It was, of course, too much to expect. The Huna were certainly cowed by the two explosions, it was the only explanation for their lack of activity, but not for long. We made it to the halfway mark and beyond in silence and then the forest foxes started to call to each other.

There was more than that, of course. The rattle of spear shafts drummed against war clubs, shrill, bird-like cries in the distance, bodies crashing through the undergrowth.

But I could hear the rushing of the river, smell the dank rottenness of it and there was hope in that.

The sounds in the undergrowth on either

side were closer now and parallel. We had a couple of hundred yards to go, no more, and there was the feeling that perhaps they were moving in for the kill.

Alberto said, 'I'll take the left, you take the right, Mallory. When I give the word let them have a couple of bursts then we all run.'

Even then, I didn't think we stood much of a chance, but there wasn't really much else we could do. I didn't hear what he shouted because he seemed to be firing that machine-pistol of his in the same instant. I swung, crouching, the Thompson gun bucking in my hands as I sprayed the foliage on my side.

We certainly hit something to judge by the cries, but I didn't stop to find out and ran like hell after Pedro and Sister Maria Teresa. For a man with an arrowhead embedded in his thigh he was doing remarkably well although I presume the prospect of what would happen to him if he fell into their hands alive was having a salutary effect.

The cries were all around us again now. I fired sideways, still running and was aware of another sound, the steady rattle of a Lewis gun.

A moment later we broke out on to the river-bank in time to see the launch moving in fast, Hannah himself working the gun in the prow.

I think it was about then that the arrows started to come, swishing through the trees one after the other, never in great numbers. One buried itself in the ground in front of me, another took Pedro full in the back, driving him forward. He spun round, took another in the chest and fell on his back.

I kept on running, ducking and weaving, for this was no place for heroes now, aware of the shooting from the launch, the hands helping Sister Maria Teresa over the rail. As Alberto followed her, an arrow pierced his left forearm. The force must have been considerable for he stumbled, dropping his Mauser into the river and I grabbed his other arm and shoved him over the rail. As I followed, I heard Hannah cry out, the engine note deepened and we started to pull away from the jetty.

Alberto staggered to his feet and in the same moment, one of his men cried out and pointed. I turned to see Pedro on his hands and knees like a dog back there on the landing stage, the stump of an arrow shaft protruding from his back. Behind him, the Huna broke from the forest howling like wolves.

Alberto snapped the shaft of the arrow in his arm with a convulsive movement, pulled it out and grabbed a rifle from the nearest man. Then he took careful aim and shot Pedro in the head.

The launch turned downstream. Alberto threw the rifle on the deck and grabbed Sister Maria Teresa by the front of her habit, shaking her in helpless rage. 'Who killed him, Sister, you or me? Tell me that? Something else for you to pray about.'

She gazed up at him mutely, a kind of horror on her face. Perhaps for the first time in her saintly life she was realising that evil as the result of good intentions is just as undesirable, but I doubt it in view of subsequent events.

As for Alberto, it was as if something went out of him. He pushed her away and said in the tiredest voice I've ever heard, 'Get away from me and stay away.'

He turned and lurched along the deck.

10

Just One of those Things

I came awake slowly, not at all certain that I was still alive and found myself in my hammock in the hangar at Landro. The kettle was boiling away on the spirit stove. Mannie was sitting beside it reading a book.

'Is it any good?' I asked him.

He turned, peering over the top of cheap spectacles at me, then closed the book, stood up and came forward, genuine concern in his eyes.

'Heh, what were you trying to do? Frighten me?'

'What happened?'

'You went out like a light, that's what

happened, just after getting out of the plane. We carted you in here and Sister Maria Teresa had a look at you.'

'What did she have to say?'

'Some kind of reaction to too much stress was all she could come up with. You crowded a lot of living into a small space in time today, boy.'

'You can say that again.'

He poured whisky into a glass – good whisky. 'Hannah?' I said.

'He's been in and out of here at least a dozen times. You've been lying there for nearly six hours. Oh, and Joanna, she was here too. Just left.'

I got out of the hammock and moved to the edge of the hangar and stared out into the night. It had stopped raining, but the air was fresh and cool, perfumed with flowers.

Piece by piece I put it all together again. Alberto's burning anger back there on the launch. He had even refused medical assistance from her – had preferred, he said, the comparatively clean hands of his medical orderly.

He had taken us straight back to the landing strip and had instructed Hannah to fly us back at once. And that just about filled in the blank pages although I couldn't for the life of me actually remember fainting.

'Coffee!' Mannie called.

I finished my whisky and took the tin mug he offered. 'Did Hannah tell you what happened up there?'

'As much as he could. Naturally there was little he could say about what took place at the actual confrontation.'

So I told him and when I was finished, he said, 'A terrible experience.'

'I'll probably dream about that walk back through the jungle for the rest of my life.'

'And this thing that took place between Sister Maria Teresa and the Colonel. A nasty business.'

'He had a point, though. If she'd done as she was told and stayed on board things might have gone differently.'

'But you can't be certain of that?'

'But she is,' I said. 'That's the trouble. Certain that whatever she does is because the good Lord has so ordained it. Certain that she's right in everything she does.'

He sighed. 'I must admit that few things are worse than a truly good person convinced they have the answer for all things.'

'A female Cromwell,' I said.

He was genuinely puzzled. 'I don't understand.'

'Read some English history, then you will. I think I'll take a walk.'

He smiled slyly. 'She will be alone, I think, except for that Huna girl she bought from Avila. The good Sister is awaiting delivery of another baby, I understand.'

'Doesn't she ever give up? What about Hannah?'

'He said he would be at the hotel.'

I found my flying jacket and walked across the landing strip towards Landro. When I reached the house, I actually paused, one foot on the bottom step of the veranda, but thought better of it.

The town itself was quiet. There was a little music through an open window from a radio and somewhere a dog barked a time or two, but otherwise there was just the night and the stars and the feeling of being alive here and now. *Here and now in this place.*

When I went up the steps to the hotel and opened the door, the bar was empty except for Hannah who sat by an open shutter, feet on the table, a bottle of whisky in front of him and a glass.

'So the dead can walk after all,' he said.

'Where is everybody?'

There had been a wedding, it seemed, a civil ceremony presided over by Figueiredo as he was empowered to do in the absence of a priest. The land agent's son, which meant there was money in it. Anyone who was anyone was at the party.

I went behind the counter and got a glass, then sat down and helped myself to whisky from his bottle. 'You satisfied now?' he said. 'After what you did back there? You feel like a man now?'

'You did a good job with the launch. Thanks.'

'No medals, kid – I've already got everything, but the Congressional. Heh, you know

235

what the Congressional is, you Limey bastard?'

I think it was only then that I realised that he had obviously drunk a great deal. I said gravely, 'Yes, I think so.'

And then he said a strange thing: 'I used to know someone just like you, Mallory, back there in the old days at the Front. We were in a Pursuit Squadron together. Fresh kid from Harvard. Old man a millionaire – all the money in the world. He couldn't take it seriously. Know what I mean?'

'I think so.'

'Hell, is that all you can say.' He filled his glass again. 'Know what he used to call me? The Black Baron on account of Von Richthofen was the Red Baron.'

'He must have thought a hell of a lot about you.'

He didn't seem to hear me. He said, 'I used to tell him, "Watch the sun. Never cross the line alone under ten thousand feet and always turn and run for home if you see a plane on its own because you can bet your sweet life it isn't."'

236

'And he didn't listen?'

'Went after a Rumpler one morning and didn't notice three F.W.s waiting upstairs in the sun. Never knew what hit him.' He shook his head. 'Silly bastard.' He looked up at me. 'But a good flyer and all the guts in the world, kid, just like you.'

His head sank on his hands, I got up and walked to the door. As I opened it he spoke without raising his head. 'Show some sense, kid. She isn't for you. We're two of a kind, her and me.'

I closed the door gently and went outside.

Light streamed out through the latticed shutters as I approached the house, golden fingers filtering into the darkness. I went up the steps to the veranda and paused. It was very quiet. Rain fluttered down, pattering on the tin roof. It was strange standing there, somehow on the outside of things, waiting for a sign that would probably never come, for the world itself to turn over.

I started to move away and on the porch a match flared pulling her face out of the darkness. There was an old cane chair up there, I had forgotten about that. She lit a cigarette and flicked the match into the night.

'Why were you going to go away?'

To find a reason or give one, was difficult, but I tried. 'I don't think there's anything here for me, that's all.'

There was a slight creaking in the darkness as she stood up. The cigarette spun through the night in a glowing arc. I was not aware that she had moved, but suddenly she was there in front of me, the scent of her like flowers in the night. She was wearing some sort of robe or housecoat, which she pulled open to hold my hands against her naked breasts.

'There's this,' she said calmly. 'Isn't that enough for you?'

It wasn't, but there was no way of explaining that, and in any event, it didn't really seem to matter. She turned, holding me by the hand and took me inside.

Naturally it was nothing like that first time, perfectly successful as a functional exercise, but no more than that. Afterwards, she was strangely discontented, which surprised me.

'What's wrong?' I demanded. 'Wasn't I up to scratch?'

'Love,' she said bitterly. 'Why does every damned man I meet have to breathe that word in my ear while he's doing it. Do you need an excuse, you men?'

Which was a hell of a thing to say and I had no answer. I got up and dressed. She pulled on her robe and went and stood at the window smoking another cigarette.

I said, 'You're a big girl now. Time you learned to tell the difference.'

I moved behind her, slipping my arms about her waist and she relaxed against me. Then she sighed, 'Too much water under the bridge. I set my sights on what I wanted a long time ago.'

'And nothing gets in the way?'

'Something like that.'

'Then what are you doing here, a thousand miles from nowhere?'

She pulled away from me and turned. 'That's different. Anna is all I've got. All that really counts.'

And she was still speaking of her in the present tense. I held her arms firmly. 'Listen to me, Joanna, you've got to face facts.'

She pulled away from me violently. 'Don't say it – don't ever say it. I don't want to hear.'

We stood there in the pale darkness confronting each other. Outside, someone called her name, there was a crash on the veranda as a chair went over. As I went into the living-room, the door burst open and Hannah staggered in. He was soaked to the skin and just about as drunk as a man could be and still stand up. He reeled back against the wall and started to slide. I grabbed him quickly.

He opened his eyes and grinned foolishly. 'Well, damn me if it isn't the boy wonder. How was it, kid? Did you manage to bring her off? When they've been around as long as she has it usually takes something special.'

No rage – no anger. I stepped back leaving him propped against the wall. Joanna said, 'Get out, Sam.'

He went down the wall in slow motion,

head lolling to one side. I was aware of Christina, the Huna girl, standing in the entrance to the other bedroom wearing a silk nightdress a couple of sizes too large for her. The eyes were very round in that flat Indian face, the skin shining like copper in the lamp-light.

Joanna stirred Hannah with her toe, then folded her arms and leaned in the open doorway. 'He's a bastard, your friend, King Size, but he knows what he's talking about. I've been a whore all my life, one way or another.'

'All right,' I said. 'Why?'

'Oh, there was Grantsville to get out of and that's the way show business is. How do you think I got where I am?'

She took the cigarette from my mouth, inhaled deeply. 'And then,' she said calmly, 'I've got to admit I like it. Always have.'

Which was honest enough, God knows, but too honest for me. I said, 'You can keep the cigarette,' and moved out into the darkness.

I paused some little distance away and

glanced back. She stood there in the doorway, silhouetted against the light, the outline of her body clear through the thin material of the housecoat. I was filled with the most damnable ache imaginable, but for what I could not be certain. Perhaps for something which had never existed in the first place?

I heard Hannah call her name faintly, she turned and closed the door. I felt a kind of release, standing there in the rain. One thing was for certain – it was the end of something.

There was news when I returned to the hangar, word over the radio that Alberto had been ordered to evacuate Santa Helena forthwith and was to pull out the following day. It touched me in no way at all, meant absolutely nothing. I ignored Mannie's troubled glances and lay in my hammock staring up at the hangar roof for the rest of the night.

I suppose it would be easy to say with hindsight that some instinct warned me that I stood on the edge of events, but certainly I was aware that something was wrong and waited, filled with a vague unease, anticipating that what was to come was not pleasant.

There was no sign of Hannah when I left at nine the following morning for Manaus on the mail run. I was tired, too tired for that game, eyes gritty from lack of sleeep and I had a hard day ahead. Not only the Manaus run, but two contract trips down-river.

Under the circumstances, I'd taken the Hayley, but the military evacuation from Santa Helena made it more than likely that Hannah would be required up there when they managed to get him out of her bed.

I made the mail drop, re-fuelled and was off again with machine parts which were needed in a hurry by one of the mining companies a hundred and fifty miles down-river and a Portuguese engineer to go with them. He wasn't at all certain about the Bristol, but I got him there in one piece and was on my way back within the hour with ore samples for the assaye officer in Manaus.

My second trip was nothing like as strenuous, a seventy-mile hop with medical supplies to a Jesuit Mission and another quick turn-about, to the great disappointment of the priest in charge, a Dutchman called Herzog who had hoped for a chess game or two and some conversation.

All in all, a rough day and it was about six o'clock in the evening when I landed again at Manaus. A couple of mechanics were waiting and I helped them get the Bristol under cover.

The de Havilland Rapide I'd noticed a day or so earlier, was parked by the end hangar again. A nice plane and as reliable as you could wish so I'd been told. The legend *Johnson Air Transport* was neatly stencilled under the cabin windows.

One of the mechanics ran me into town in the old Crossley tender again. I dozed off in the cab and had to be awakened when we reached the Palace. Hardly surprising, when you consider that I hadn't slept at all the previous night.

I wanted a drink badly. I also needed about twelve hours in bed. I hesitated by the reception desk, considering the matter. The need for a very large brandy won hands down and

I went into the bar. If I hadn't, things might have turned out very differently, but then, most of life, or what it becomes, depends upon such turns.

A small, wiry man in flying boots and leather jacket sat on the end stool constructing a tower of toothpicks on the base of an upturned glass. There was no barman as usual. I dropped my grip on the floor, went behind the counter and found a bottle of Courvoisier.

His left eye was fixed for all time, a reasonable facsimile of the real thing in glass. The face was expressionless, a wax-like film of scar tissues, and when he spoke the mouth didn't seem to move at all.

'Jack Johnson,' he said in a hard Australian twang. 'Not that I'm any bloody punch-up artist like the black fella.'

I held up the brandy bottle, he nodded and I reached for another glass. 'That your Rapide up on the field?'

'That's it, sport, Johnson Air Transport. Sounds pretty good, eh?'

'Sounds bloody marvellous,' I said and stuck out my hand. 'Neil Mallory.'

'Well, I'll come clean. That Rapide is Johnson Air Transport.' He frowned suddenly. 'Mallory? Say, are you the bloke who's been flying that old Bristol for the Baron?'

'The Baron?' I said.

'Sam Hannah, the Black Baron. That's what we used to call him at the Front during the war. I was out there with the R.F.C.'

'You knew him well?'

'Hell, everybody knew the Black Baron. He was hot stuff. One of the best there was.'

So it was all true, every damned word and I had been convinced he had told me some private fantasy of long ago, a tissue of half-truths and exaggerations.

'But that was in another country, as they say,' Johnson went on. 'Poor old Sam's been on the long slide to nowhere ever since. By God, his luck certainly turned when you came along. You saved his bacon and no mistake. I hope he's paying you right?'

'The boot was on the other foot,' I said. 'If he hadn't taken me on when he did, I'd have ended up on the labour gang. He already had another pilot lined when I arrived.'

It was difficult to come to terms with that face of his. There was no way of knowing what was going on behind the mask. There was just that hard Australian voice. In other words, he gave nothing away and to this day I am still not certain whether what happened was by accident or design.

He said, 'What other pilot? What are you talking about?'

'Portuguese, I think. I don't know his name. I believe he'd been flying for a mining company in Venezuela which went bust.'

'First I've heard of it and pilots are like gold on the Amazon these days, what with the Spanish war and all this trouble coming up in Europe. You must have seemed like manna from heaven to poor old Sam dropping in like that after all those bad breaks he had. But he sure ran it close. A week left to get a second plane airborne and Charlie Wilson waiting to fly up from Belem and take over his government contract.'

'Charlie Wilson?' I said.

'Haven't you met Charlie?' He helped himself to another brandy. 'Nice bloke – Canadian – works the lower end of the river out of Belem with three Rapides. Sell his sister if he had to. Mind you I always thought Sam would come up with something. Nobody in his right mind is going to let twenty thousand dollars slip through his fingers that easily.'

It was all turning over inside me now, currents pulling every which-way, explanations for some irrational things which had never made any sense rising to the surface.

'Twenty thousand dollars?' I said carefully.

'Sure, his bonus.'

'I hadn't realised it was as much as that.'

'I should know. I bid for the contract myself originally then my partner went West in our other plane so that was that. I've been free-lancing since then in the middle section of the river operating from Colona about four hundred miles from here. I don't get into Manaus often.'

He went on talking, but I didn't hear for I had other things on my mind. I went round the counter, picked up my canvas grip and moved to the door.

'See you around, sport,' Johnson called.

I suppose I made some sort of answer, but I can't be certain for I was too busy reliving that first night in minutest detail. My meeting with Hannah, events at *The Little Boat*, Maria of the Angels and what had happened later.

For the first time, or at least for the first time consciously, it occurred to me that, to use one of Hannah's favourite phrases, I had been taken.

Strange how the body reacts according to circumstances. Sleep was the least of my requirements now. What I needed were answers and it seemed a reasonable assumption that I might get them at the place where it had all started.

I had a cold bath, mainly to sharpen myself up for it had occurred to me that I might well need my wits about me before the night was over. Then I dressed in my linen suit, creased as it was from packing, slipped the

.45 automatic in one pocket, a handful of cartridges in the other and left.

It was eight o'clock when I reached *The Little Boat*, early by their standards and there wasn't much happening. I wanted one person, Hannah's old girl-friend, Lola of the red satin dress, and she was not there. Would not be in until nine-thirty at the earliest according to the barman.

I steeled myself to wait as patiently as possible. I'd had no more than a sandwich all day so I went out on the private deck and ordered dinner and a bottle of Pouilly on Hannah's account which gave me a perverse pleasure.

Lola arrived rather earlier than expected. I was at the coffee stage of things when the sliding door opened then closed again behind me, fingers gently ruffled my hair and she moved round to the other side of the table.

She looked surprisingly respectable for once in a well-fitting black skirt and a white cotton blouse which buttoned down the front.

'Tomas says you were asking for me.' She pushed a glass towards me. 'Any special reason?'

I filled her glass. 'I was looking for a little fun, that's all. I'm in for the night.'

'And Sam?'

'What about Sam?'

'He is with this – this woman who was here the other night? The American?'

'Oh, she seems to have become something of a permanent fixture up at Landro,' I said.

The stem of the wineglass snapped in her hand. 'God damn him to hell,' she said bitterly.

'I know how you feel,' I said. 'I love him too.'

She frowned instantly. 'What do you mean?'

I stamped on the floor for the waiter. 'Oh, come on now,' I said. 'Maria of the Angels, you remember her? The one who was so good at dropping out of sight? Mean to say you and Hannah had never clapped eyes on her before?'

The waiter appeared with another bottle. She said carefully, 'And even if this were so, why should I tell you?'

'To get your own back on him. Much simpler from your point of view than sticking a knife in his back. Now that can be messy. That would get you at least ten years.'

She laughed out loud, spilling her wine on the table. 'You know, I like you, Englishman. I like you a lot.'

She leaned across the table, her mouth opening as she kissed me, tongue probing. After a reasonably lengthy interval, she eased away. Her smile had faded slightly and there was a look of surprise on her face. She seemed to come to some decision and patted my cheek.

'I'll make a bargain with you. You give me what I want and I'll tell you what you want. A deal?'

'All right,' I said automatically.

'Good. My place is just along the water-front from here.'

She walked out and I followed, wondering what in the hell I'd let myself in for now.

The room was surprisingly clean with a balcony overlooking the river, the image of the Virgin and Child on the wall above a flickering candle. Lola herself was a surprise to say the least. She left me on the balcony with a drink and disappeared for a good fifteen minutes. When she returned, she was wearing a housecoat in plain blue silk. Every trace of make-up had been scrubbed from her face and she had tied back her hair.

I got up and put down my glass. She stood looking at me for a while then took off the housecoat and threw it on the bed. Few women are seen at their best in the nude. She had a body to thank God for.

She stood there, hands on hips, and said calmly, 'I am beautiful, Senhor Mallory?'

'Few men would dispute that.'

'But I am a whore,' she said flatly. 'Beautiful perhaps, but still a whore. Available to any man who can raise the price.'

I thought of Joanna Martin who had never actually taken cash on the barrel which was the only difference between them.

'And I am tired of it all,' she said. 'Just for once I would like a man who can be honest with me as I am honest with him. Who will not simply use me. You understand?'

'I think so,' I said.

She blew out the light.

It was late when I awakened. Just after two a.m. according to the luminous dial of my watch. I was alone in the bed, but when I turned my head I saw the glow of her cigarette out there on the terrace.

I started to get dressed. She called softly, 'You are leaving?'

'I'll have to,' I said. 'I've things to do or had you forgotten?'

There was silence for a while and then, as I pulled on my boots, she said, 'There is a street opposite the last pier at the other end of the waterfront from here. The house, on the corner has a lion carved over the door. You want the apartment at the top of the second flight of stairs.'

I pulled on my jacket. 'And what will I find there?'

'I wouldn't dream of spoiling the surprise.'

I moved to the door, uncertain of what to say. She said, 'Will you be back?'

'I don't think it very likely.'

'Honest to the last,' she said rather bitterly, then laughed, sounding for the first time since we had left *The Little Boat* like the old Lola. 'And in the end, Senhor Mallory, I'm not at all certain that was what I really wanted. Don't you find that rather amusing?'

Which I didn't and did what I suspected was the best thing in the circumstances and got out of there fast.

I found the house with the lion above the door easily enough. It was one of those baroque monstrosities left over from the last century, probably built for some wealthy merchant and now in a state of what one might delicately term multiple occupation. The front door opened at once giving access to a large gloomy hall illuminated by a single oil lamp. There was a party going on in one of the downstairs back rooms, I heard a burst of noise and music as someone opened and closed a door.

I started up the stairs in the silence which followed. The first landing was illuminated like the hall below by a single oil lamp, but the next flight of stairs disappeared into darkness.

I went up cautiously, feeling my way along the wall, aware of the patter of tiny feet as the rats and lizards scattered out of the way. When I reached the landing, I struck a match and held it above my head. There was no name on the door opposite and the lamp on the wall was cold.

The match started to burn my fingers so I dropped it and tried the door handle with infinite caution. It was locked so I did the obvious thing and knocked gently.

After a while, a lamp was turned up, light seeping under the door, there was movement, a man's voice and then a woman. Someone shuffled towards the door, I knocked again.

'Who is it?' the woman demanded.

'Lola sent me,' I answered in Portuguese.

The door started to open, I moved back into the shadows. She said, 'Look, I've got someone with me at the moment. Can't you come back a little later?'

I didn't reply. The door opened even wider

and Maria of the Angels peered out. 'Heh, where are you man?'

I took her by the throat, stifling all sound, and ran her back into the room, shutting the door quietly behind. The man in the bed, who cried out in alarm, was a mountain of flesh if ever I've seen one. A great quivering jelly more likely to die of fright than anything else.

I produced the .45 and waved it at him. 'Keep your mouth shut and you won't get hurt.'

Then I turned to Maria. 'I'd have thought you could have done better than that.'

She was calmer now, a trifle arrogant even. She pulled the old wrapper she was wearing closer around her and folded her arms. 'What do you want?'

'Answers, that's all. Tell me what I want to know and I won't bring the police into this.'

'The police?' She laughed at that one. Then shrugged. 'All right, Senhor Mallory, ask away.'

'It was a set-up our meeting that night, arranged by Hannah – am I right?'

'I'd just come up-river,' she said. 'I was new in town. Nobody knew me except Lola. We're second cousins.'

'What did he pay you?'

'He told me to take whatever money was in your wallet and get rid of anything else.'

The instant she said it, I knew that she had not done as she was told. She wasn't the sort. I said, 'You've still got them, haven't you? My wallet and the passport.'

She sighed in a kind of impatience, turned to a sideboard, opened the drawer and took out my wallet. The passport was inside together with a few other bits and pieces and a photo of my mother and father. I was caught by that for a moment then stowed it away and put the wallet in my breast pocket.

'Your parents, senhor?' I nodded. 'They look nice people. You will not go to the police?'

I shook my head and put the .45 back in my pocket. 'That's one hell of a knee you have there.'

'It's a hard world, senhor.'

'You can say that again.'

I let myself out and went down the stairs. It was very quiet on the waterfront and I walked along the pier and sat on a rail at the end smoking a cigarette, feeling absurdly calm in the circumstances.

It was as if I had always known and had not wanted to face it and perhaps that was so. But now it was out in the open. Now came the reckoning.

I got up and walked back along the pier, footsteps booming hollowly on the wooden flooring, echoing into the night.

11

Showdown

I had a contract run to make at nine o'clock, a mail pick-up which meant it could not be avoided. It was a tedious run. Sixty miles down-river, another fifty to a trading post at the headwaters of a small tributary to the west.

I cut it down to sixty-five miles by taking the shortest route between two points and flying across country over virgin jungle. A crazy thing to do and asking for trouble, but it meant I could do the round trip in a couple of hours. A brief pause to re-fuel in Manaus and I could be on my way to Landro by noon. Perhaps because of that, the elements decided to take a hand and I flew into Manaus, thunder echoing on the horizon like distant drums.

The rain started as I landed, an instant downpour that closed my world down to a very small compass indeed. I taxied to the hangar and the mechanics ran out in rubber ponchos and helped me get her inside.

The mail was waiting for me, they re-fuelled her quickly enough, but afterwards I could do nothing except stand at the edge of the hangar smoking cigarette after cigarette, staring out at the worst downpour since the rainy season.

After my meeting with Maria of the Angels I had felt surprisingly calm in spite of her story. For most of the morning I'd had things well under control, but now, out of very frustration, I wanted to get to Landro so badly that I could taste it. Wanted to see Hannah's face when I produced my wallet and pass-port, confronted him with the evidence of his treachery. From the start of things I had never really cared for him. Now it was a question of hate more than anything else and it was nothing to do with Joanna Martin.

Looking back on it all I think that what stuck in my throat most was the feeling that he had used me quite deliberately to further his own ends all along the line. There was a kind of contempt in that which did not sit easy.

According to the radio the situation at Landro was no better, so more for something to do than anything else, I borrowed the Crossley tender, drove into town and had a meal at a fish restaurant on the waterfront.

At the bar afterwards and halfway through my second large brandy, I became aware of a stranger staring out at me from the mirror opposite.

Small for his size as my grandmother used to say, long arms, large hands, but a hard, tough, competent-looking young man or was that only what I wanted to believe? The leather flying jacket gaped satisfactorily revealing the .45 automatic in the chest holster, the mark of the true adventurer, but the weary young face had to be seen to be believed.

Was this all I had to show for two long years? Was this what I'd left home for?

I looked down through the rain at a stern-wheeler making ready to leave for the coast. It came to me then that I could leave now. Leave it all. Book passage using Hannah's famous credit system. Once in Belem I would be all right. I had a passport again. I could always work my passage to Europe from there. Something would turn up.

I rejected the thought as instantly as I had considered it. There was something here that had to be worked through to the end and I was a part of it. To go now would be to leave the story unfinished like a novel with the end pages missing and the memory of him would haunt me for the rest of my life. I had to lay Hannah's ghost personally, there could be no other way.

The rain still fell in a heavy grey curtain as I drove back to the airstrip and so continued for the rest of the afternoon. Most serious of all, by four o'clock the surface had turned into a thick, glutinous mud that would get worse before it got better. Much more of this and it would be like trying to take off in a ploughed field.

Another half-hour and it was obvious that if I did not go then I would not get away at all, had probably left it too late already. I told the mechanics it was now or never and got ready to leave.

I started the engine while still inside the hangar and gave it plenty of time to warm up, an essential factor under the circumstances. When I taxied out into the open, the force of the rain had to be felt to be believed. At the very best it was going to be an uncomfortable run.

The strip was five hundred yards long. Usually two hundred was ample for the Bristol's take-off but not today. My tail skidded from side to side, the thick mud sucked at the wheels, showering up in great fountains.

At two hundred yards, I hadn't even managed to raise the tail, at two-fifty I was convinced I was wasting my time, had better quit while still ahead and take her back to the hangar. And then, at three hundred and for no logical reason that I could see, the tail came up. I brought the stick back gently and we lifted into the grey curtain.

* * *

It took me two hours but I made it. Two hours of hell, for the rain and the dense mist it produced from the warm earth covered the jungle and river alike in a grey blanket, producing some of the worst flying conditions I have ever known.

To stay with the river with anything like certainty, I had to fly at fifty feet for most of the way, a memorable experience for at that altitude, if that is what it can be termed, there was no room for even the slightest error in judgement and the radio had packed in, (the rain, as it turned out,) which didn't help in the final stages, for conditions at Landro were no better than they had been at Manaus.

But by then I'd had it. I was soaked to the skin, bitterly cold and suffering badly from cramp in both legs. As I came abreast of the airstrip, Mannie ran out from the hangar. Everything looked as clear as it was ever going to be so I simply banked in over the trees and dropped her down.

It was a messy business, all hands and feet. The Bristol bounced once, then the tail slewed round and we skidded forward on what seemed like the crest of a muddy brown wave.

When I switched off, the silence was beautiful. I sat there plastered with mud from head to toe, the engine still sounding inside my head.

Mannie arrived a few seconds later. He climbed up on the lower port wing and peered over the edge of the cockpit, a look of awe on his face. 'You must be mad,' he said. 'Why did you do it?'

'A kind of wild justice, Mannie, isn't that what Bacon called it?' He stared at me, puzzled as I stood and flung a leg over the edge of the cockpit. 'Revenge, Mannie. Revenge.'

But by then I was no longer in control, which was understandable enough. I started to laugh weakly, slid to the ground and fell headlong into the mud.

I sat at the table in the hangar wrapped in a couple of blankets, a glass of whisky in my hands and watched him make coffee over the spirit stove.

'Where's Hannah?'

267

'At the hotel as far as I know. There was a message over the radio from Figueiredo to say he wouldn't be back till the morning because of the weather.'

'Where is he?'

'Fifteen miles up-river, that's all Trouble at one of the villages.'

I finished the whisky and he handed me a mug of coffee. 'What is it, Neil?' he said gravely. 'What's happened?'

I answered him with a question. 'Tell me something? Hannah's bonus at the end of the contract? How much?'

'Five thousand dollars.' There was a quick wariness in his eyes as he said it and I wondered why.

I shook my head. 'Twenty, Mannie.'

There was a short silence. He said, 'That isn't possible.'

'All things are in this best of all possible worlds, isn't that what they say? Even miracles, it seems.'

I took out my wallet and passport and threw them on the table. 'I found her, Mannie – the girl who robbed me that night

268

at *The Little Boat* – robbed me because Hannah needed me broke and in trouble. There was never any Portuguese pilot. If I hadn't turned up when I did he would have been finished.'

The breath went out from him like wind through the branches of a tree on a quiet evening. He slumped into the opposite chair, staring down at the wallet and passport.

After a while he said, 'What are you going to do?'

'I don't know. Finish this coffee then go and show him those. Should produce an interesting reaction.'

'All right,' Mannie said. 'So he was wrong. He shouldn't have treated you that way. But, Neil, this was his last chance. He was a desperate man faced with the final end of things. No excuse, perhaps, but it at least makes what he did understandable.'

'Understandable?' I stood up, allowing the blankets to slip to the ground, almost choking on my anger. 'Mannie, I've got news for you. I'll see that bastard in hell for what he's done to me.'

269

I picked up the wallet and passport, turned and plunged out into the rain.

I hadn't the slightest idea what I was going to do when I saw him. In a way, I was living from minute to minute. I'd had virtually no sleep for two nights now, remember, and things seemed very much to be happening in slow motion.

As I came abreast of the house I saw the Huna girl, Christina, standing on the porch watching me. I thought for a moment that Joanna or the good Sister might appear, not that it would have mattered.

I kept on going, putting one foot doggedly in front of the other. I must have presented an extraordinary sight, my face and clothing streaked with mud, painted for war like a Huna, soaked to the skin. People stopped talking on the verandas of the houses as I passed and several ragged children ran out into the rain and followed behind me, jabbering excitedly.

As I approached the hotel I heard singing and recognised the tune immediately, a song I'd heard often sung by some of the old R.F.C.

hands round the mess piano on those R.A.F. Auxiliary weekend courses.

I was damned if I could remember the title, another proof of how tired I was. My name sounded clear through the rain as I reached the bottom of the hotel steps. I turned and found Mannie hurrying up the street.

'Wait for me, Neil,' he called, but I ignored him, went up the steps to the veranda, nodded to Avila and a couple of men who were lounging there and went inside.

Joanna Martin and Sister Maria Teresa sat at a table by the window drinking coffee. Figueiredo's wife stood behind the bar. Hannah sat on a stool at the far end, head back, singing for all he was worth.

> *So stand by your glasses steady,*
> *This world is a world of lies:*
> *A cup to the dead already*
> *Hurrah for the next man who dies.*

He had, as the Irish say, drink taken, but he was far from drunk and his voice was surprisingly good. As the last notes died away the two women applauded, Sister Maria Teresa beaming enthusiastically, although the look on Joanna's face was more one of indulgence than anything else – and then she saw me and the eyes widened.

The door was flung open behind me as Mannie arrived. He was short of breath, his face grey, and clutched a shotgun to his chest.

Hannah said, 'Well, damn me, you look like something the cat brought in. What happened?'

Mannie grabbed my arm. 'No trouble, Neil.'

I pulled free, went along the bar slowly. Hannah's smile didn't exactly fade away, it simply froze into place, fixed like a death mask. When I was close I took out the wallet and passport and threw them on the bar.

'I ran into an old friend of yours last night, Sam.'

He picked up the wallet, considered it for a moment. 'If this is yours I'm certainly glad you've got it back, but I can't say I know what in the hell you're talking about.'

'Just tell me one thing,' I said. 'The bonus. For five thousand read twenty, am I right?'

Joanna Martin moved into view. 'What is all this?'

I stiff-armed her out of the way and he didn't like that, anger sparking in those blue eyes, the smile slipping. The solution, when it came, was so beautifully simple. I picked up the passport and wallet and stowed them away.

'I'll do the Manaus mail run in the morning as usual,' I said. 'You can manage without me after that. I'll leave the Bristol there.'

I started to turn away. He grabbed me by the arm and jerked me round to face him again. 'Oh, no you don't. We've got a contract.'

'I know; signed, sealed, delivered. You can wipe your backside on it as far as I'm concerned.'

I think it was only then that he realised just how much trouble he was in. He said hoarsely, 'But I've got to keep two planes in the air, kid, you know that. If I don't, those bastards in Belem invoke the penalty clause. I'll lose that bonus. Everything. I'm in hock

273

up to my ears. They could even take the Hayley.'

'Marvellous,' I said. 'I hope that means they keep you here for ever. I hope you never get out of this stinking hole.'

He hit me then, a good, solid punch that caught me high on the cheek, sending me back against the bar, glasses crashing to the floor.

I have never been much of a fighting man. The idea of getting into the ring to have your face reduced to pulp by a more skilful boxer than yourself just to show you're a man has always struck me as a poor kind of sport, but the life I had been living for the past two years had taught me a thing or two.

I lashed out with my left foot, catching him under the knee. He cried out and doubled over so I gave him my knee in the face for good measure.

He went back over a cane table with a crash. Both women cried out, there was a considerable amount of confused shouting which meant nothing to me for I had blood in my eye now with a vengeance.

I jumped on him as he started to get up and found him in better shape than he deserved, but then, I had forgotten that colossal strength of his. I got a fist under the ribs that almost took my breath away, another in the face and then my hands fastened around his throat.

We turned over and over, tearing at each other like a couple of mad dogs and then there was a deafening explosion that had us rolling apart in an instant.

Mannie stood over us clutching the shotgun, his face very pale. 'Enough is enough,' he said. 'No more of this stupidity.'

In the silence, I was aware of Avila and his friends outside on the terrace peering in, of the anguish on Sister Maria Teresa's face, of Joanna Martin, watchful and somehow wary, glancing first at Hannah and then at me.

We got to our feet together. 'All right, have it your way, Mannie, but I'm still clearing out in the morning.'

'We've got a contract.' It was a cry of agony and Hannah swayed, clutching at the table, blood streaming from his nose which, as I discovered later, I had broken with my knee.

I jerked my thumb at the shotgun. 'I've got one of those too, Sam, remember? Try and stop me leaving in the morning and I'm just liable to use it.'

When I turned and walked out, nobody got in my way.

It was growing dark as I ploughed my way back through the hangar. I lit the lamp and poured another whisky. I put my head on my hands and closed my eyes and fireworks sparked off in the darkness. My legs ached, my face ached. I wanted nothing so much as sleep.

I sat up and found Joanna Martin standing at the edge of the hangar looking at me. We stared at each other in silence for quite some time. Finally I said, 'Did he send you?'

'If you do this to him he's finished,' she replied.

'I'd say he's just about earned it.'

Anger flared up in her suddenly. 'Who in the hell do you think you are, Lord God

Almighty? Haven't you ever made a mistake? The guy was desperate. He's sorry for what he's done. He'll make it up to you.'

I said, 'What are you supposed to do next? Take me back to bed?'

She turned and walked out. I sat there staring into the darkness, listening to the rain and Mannie moved out of the shadows.

'You too?' I said. 'What are you going to do? Tell me some cosy Hassidic story about some saintly old rabbi who always turned the other cheek and smiled gratefully when they spat on him?'

I don't know whether he'd come with the intention of appealing to me to think again. If he had, then that little speech of mine made him certainly think twice. He simply said, 'I think you're wrong, Neil, taking all the circumstances into account, but it's your decision,' and he turned and followed Joanna Martin.

By then I not only didn't give a damn, I was past caring about anything. I was getting out and nothing on this earth was going to stop me. Let that be an end of it.

I changed into dry clothes, climbed into my hammock, hitched a blanket around my shoulders and was almost instantly asleep.

I don't know what time the rain stopped, but I awakened to a beautiful morning at eight o'clock, having slept for twelve solid hours. I was sore all over and cramp, that occupational disease of pilots, grabbed at my legs as I sat up. My face ached and I peered in the mirror Mannie had fixed to one of the roof posts; I saw that both cheeks were badly swollen and discoloured with bruising.

There was a step behind me and Mannie appeared, wiping his hands on some cotton waste. He was wearing his overalls and there was grease on his face. The Bristol was parked out on the airstrip.

'How do you feel?' he asked.

'Terrible. Is there any coffee?'

'Ready on the stove. Just needs heating.'

I turned up the flame. 'What have you been doing?'

'My job,' he said calmly. 'You've got a mail run this morning, haven't you?'

'That's right,' I said deliberately.

He nodded towards the Bristol. 'There she is. Ready and waiting for you.'

He turned away. I poured myself a mug of coffee and got ready to go. I had just finished packing my grip for the last time when Hannah arrived.

He looked terrible, the face badly bruised, the nose obviously out of alignment and the eyes were washed clean of all feeling. He wore his leather boots, breeches and an old khaki shirt, a white scarf looped around his neck. He carried the mail sack in his left hand.

He said calmly, 'Are you still going through with this?'

'What do you think?'

'Okay,' he said, still calm. 'Suit yourself.'

He walked across to the Bristol, climbed up and stowed the sack in the observer's cockpit. I followed slowly, my grip in one hand, zipping up my jacket with the other.

Mannie stayed in the hangar, which didn't make me feel too good, but if that was the way he wanted it, then to hell with him. Quite suddenly I had an overwhelming desire to get away from that place. I'd had Landro, I'd had Brazil.

I put my foot on the lower port wing and climbed into the cockpit. Hannah waited patiently while I fastened my helmet and went through my checks. He reached for the propeller, I began to wind the starting magneto and gave him the signal. And then he did a totally unexpected thing. He smiled or at least I think that's what it was supposed to be and called, 'Happy landings, kid.' Then he pulled the propeller.

It almost worked. I fought against the impulse to cut the engine, turned into the wind before I could change my mind and took off. As I banked across the trees the government launch moved in to the jetty, Figueiredo standing in the stern. He waved his hat to me, I waved back, took a final look at Landro then turned south.

I had a good fast run and raised Manaus in an hour and forty minutes. There were a couple of cars parked by the tower as I came in. A rather imposing black Mercedes and an

Oldsmobile. As I taxied towards the hangar, they started up and moved towards me. When I stopped, so did they.

A uniformed policeman slid from behind the wheel of a Mercedes and opened the rear door for the *comandante* who waved cheerfully and called a good morning. Three more policemen got out of the Oldsmobile, all armed to the teeth. *Hannah and that damned contract of ours.* So this was why he had been so cheerful?

I slid to the ground and took the hand the *comandante* so genially held out to me. 'What's this? I don't usually rate a guard of honour.'

His eyes behind the dark glasses gave nothing away. 'A small matter. I won't keep you long, my friend. Tell me, Senhor Figueiredo has a safe at his place of business, you are aware of this?'

I knew at once that it was about as bad as it could be. I said, 'Along with everyone else in Landro. It's under the bar counter.'

'And the key? I understand Senhora Figueiredo can be regrettably careless regarding its whereabouts.'

'Something else well known to everyone in Landro,' I said. 'She hangs it behind the bar. Look – what is this?'

'I had a message from Senhor Figueiredo over the radio half an hour ago to say that when he opened his safe this morning to check the contents after his absence, he discovered a consignment of uncut diamonds was missing.'

I took a deep breath. 'Now, look here,' I said. 'Any one of fifty people could have taken them. Why pick on me?'

He nodded briefly, three of the policemen crowded in on me, the fourth climbed up into the observer's cockpit and threw out the mail sack and my grip which the *comandante* started to search. The man in the cockpit said something briefly in Portuguese that I couldn't catch and handed down a small canvas bag.

'Yours, senhor?' the *comandante* inquired politely.

'I've never seen it before in my life.'

He opened the bag, peered inside briefly, then poured a stream of uncut diamonds into his left palm.

* * *

There was a terrible inevitability to it all after that, but I didn't go down without a struggle. The *comandante* didn't question me himself – not at first. I told my story from beginning to end and exactly as it had happened, to a surprisingly polite young lieutenant who wrote it all down and made no comment.

Then I was taken downstairs to a cell that was almost a parody of what you expected to find up-country in backward South American republics. There were at least forty of us crammed into a space fit for half that number. One bucket for urine, another for excrement and a smell that had to be experienced to be believed.

Most of the others were the sort who were too poor to buy themselves out of trouble. Indians in the main, of the kind who had come to town to learn the white man's big secret and who had found only poverty and degradation.

I pushed towards the window and most of them got out of my way respectfully out of sheer habit. A large, powerful-looking Negro in a crumpled linen suit and straw sombrero sat on a bench against the wall. He looked capable of most things and certainly when he barked an order, the two Indians sitting beside him got out of the way fast enough.

He smiled amiably. 'You have a cigarette for me, senhor?'

As it happened, I had a spare packet in one of my pockets and he seized them avidly. I had a distinct feeling I had made the right gesture.

He said, 'What have they pulled you in for, my friend?'

'A misunderstanding, that's all,' I told him. 'I'll be released before the day's out.'

'As God wills, senhor.'

'And you?'

'I killed a man. They called it manslaughter because my wife was involved, you understand? That was six months ago. I was sentenced by the court yesterday. Three years at hard labour.'

'I suppose it could have been worse,' I said. 'Better than hanging.'

'It is all one in the end, senhor,' he said

with a kind of indifference. 'They are sending me to Machados.'

I couldn't think of a thing to say, for the very name was enough to frighten most people locally. A labour camp in the middle of a swamp two or three hundred miles from nowhere on the banks of the Negro. The sort of place from which few people seemed to return.

I said, 'I'm sorry about that.'

He smiled sadly, tilted his hat over his eyes and leaned back against the wall.

I stood at the window which gave a ground-level view of the square at the front of the building. There weren't many people about, just a couple of horse-drawn cabs waiting for custom, drivers dozing in the hot sun. It was peaceful out there. I decided this must all be a dream, that I'd waken very soon and then the Crossley tender from the airstrip pulled up at the bottom of the steps and Hannah got out.

They came for me about two hours later, took me upstairs and left me outside the *comandante's* office with a couple of guards. After a while, the door opened and Hannah and the *comandante* emerged, shaking hands affably.

'You have been more than helpful, my friend,' the *comandante* said. 'A sad business.'

Hannah turned and saw me. His face looked worse than ever for the bruising had deepened, but an expression of real concern appeared for all to see and he strode forward, ignoring the *comandante's* hand on his shoulder.

'For God's sake, kid, why did you do it?'

I tried to take a swing at him and both guards grappled with me at once. 'Please, Captain Hannah,' the *comandante* said. 'Better to go now.'

He took him firmly to the outer door and Hannah, a look of agony on his face now, called, 'Anything, kid – anything I can do. Just ask.'

The *comandante* returned to his office, leaving the door ajar. After a couple of minutes, he called for me and the guards took me in. He sat at his desk examining a typed document for a while.

'Your statement.' He held it up. 'Is there anything you wish to change?'

'Not a word.'

'Then you will please sign it. Please read it through first.'

I found it a fair and accurate account of what I had said, something to be surprised at, and signed it.

He put it on one side, lit a cigarillo and sat back. 'Right, Senhor Mallory, facts only from now on. You have made certain accusations against my good friend Captain Hannah who, I may say, flew down especially at my request to make a statement.'

'In which he naturally denies everything.'

'I do not have to take his word for anything. The woman, Lola Coimbra – I have interviewed her personally. She rejects your story completely.'

I was sorry about that, in spite of my position – sorry for Lola more than for myself.

'And this woman Maria,' he went on. 'The one you say assaulted you. Would it surprise you to know she is not known at the address you give?'

By then, of course, I had got past being surprised at anything, but still struggled to keep afloat. 'Then where did I get the wallet and passport from?'

'Who knows, senhor? Perhaps you've never been parted from them. Perhaps the whole affair was an elaborate plot on your part to gain Captain Hannah's sympathy so that he would offer you employment.'

Which took the wind right out of my sails. I struggled for words and said angrily, 'None of this would stand up in a court of law for five minutes.'

'Which is for the court to decide. Leaving all other considerations on one side, there is no question in my mind that you have a clear case to answer on the charge of being in unlawful possession of uncut diamonds to the value of . . .' Here, he checked a document before him. 'Yes, sixty thousand *cruzeiros*.'

Round about nine thousand pounds. I swallowed hard. 'All right. I want to be put in touch with the British Consul in Belem and I'll need a lawyer.'

'There will be plenty of time for that.'

He reached for an official-looking document

with a seal at the bottom and signed it. I said, 'What's that supposed to mean?'

'The courts are under great pressure, my friend. This is a wild region. There are many wrong-doers. The scum of Brazil run here to hide. It may be at least six months before your case is heard.'

I couldn't believe my ears. I said, 'What the hell are you talking about?'

He carried on as if I had not spoken. 'For the present, you will be committed to the labour camp at Machados until your case comes to trial. As it happens a new batch of prisoners go up-river in the morning.'

He dismissed me, nodding at the guards to take me away, the last straw as far as I was concerned. 'Listen to me, damn you!' I reached across the desk, grabbing him by the front of the tunic.

It was about the worst thing I could have done. One of the guards jabbed the end of his club into my kidneys and I went down like a stone. Then they grabbed an arm each and took me down the two flights of stairs to the basement between them, feet dragging.

I was vaguely aware of the door of the cell being opened, of being thrown inside. I passed out for a while then and surfaced to find my Negro friend squatting beside me.

He held a lighted cigarette to my lips, his face expressionless. 'The misunderstanding – it still exists?'

'I think you could say that,' I told him weakly. 'They're sending me to Machados in the morning.'

He took it very philosophically. 'Have courage, my friend. Sometimes God looks down through the clouds.'

'Not today,' I said.

I think the night which followed was the lowest point of my life, but the final humiliation was still to come. On the following morning, just before noon, the Negro, whose name turned out rather improbably to be Munro, a legacy from some Scottish plantation owner in the past, myself and about thirty other prisoners were taken out to the yard at the back to be fitted with leg and wrist irons for the trip up-river.

There was absolutely nothing to be done

about it. I simply had to accept for the moment like everyone else and yet when the sergeant in charge got to me and screwed the ankle bracelets up tight, it seemed like the final nail in my coffin.

Just after that it started to rain. They left us standing in the open for another hour, during which we got soaked to the skin, unnecessary cruelty but the sort of thing to be expected from now on. Finally, we were formed into a column and marched away at a brisk shuffle towards the docks.

There was a café and bar at the corner of the square and there were plenty of people sitting on the veranda having coffee and an aperitif before lunch. Most of them stood up to get a good view as we went past, chains clanking.

Hannah's face jumped out at me instantly for although he was standing at the back of the crowd, he was easily visible because of his height. He had a glass of something or other in his right hand, actually raised it in a silent toast, then turned away and strolled casually inside.

12

Hell on Earth

We were three days in the hold of an old stern-wheeler that worked its way up-river once a week, calling at every village on the way with a jetty large enough to lay alongside. Most people travelled on deck, sleeping in hammocks because of the heat. The guards let us up once a day for air, usually in the evening, but in spite of that two of the older men died.

One of the prisoners, a small man with skin like dried-up leather and hair that was prematurely white, had already served seven months at Machados while awaiting trial. He painted a harrowing picture of a kind of hell on earth, a charnel house where the whip was the order of the day and men died like flies from ill-treatment and disease.

But for me the present was enough. A nightmare, no reality to it at all. I found myself a dark little corner of my own and crouched there for two days in a kind of stupor, unable to believe that this was really happening to me. It was real enough, God knows and the pain and the squalor and the hunger of it could not be evaded. It existed in every cruel detail and it was Hannah who had put me here.

Munro had done his best with me during this period, patiently continuing to talk, even when I refused to answer, feeding me cigarettes until the packet I'd given him was empty. In the end, he gave up the struggle in a kind of disgust and I recalled his final words clearly as he got up and shuffled away.

'Forgive me, senhor, I can see I've been talking to a man who is already dead.'

It took a dead man to bring me back to life. On the evening of the third day I was awakened by the sound of the hatch being opened. There was a general movement instantly, everyone eager to be the first out into the clean air. The man next to me still slept on, leaning heavily against me, his head on my shoulder. I shoved him away and he went over in slow motion and lay still.

Munro pushed his way through the press and went down on his knees. After a while he shrugged and scrambled to his feet. 'He's been dead for two or three hours.'

My flesh crawled, I felt in some indefinable way unclean for it was as if death in taking this man had touched me also. Someone called out and a guard came down the ladder. He checked the body casually then nodded to Munro and me. 'You two – get him on deck.'

Munro said, 'I'll get on my knees and you put him over my shoulder. It's the easiest way.'

He got down and I stood there, trapped by the horror of it all, filled with unutterable loathing at the idea of even touching that body.

The guard belted me across the shoulder blades with his club, the usual careless brutality. 'Get moving, we haven't got all day.'

Somehow I got the body across Munro's shoulders, followed him up the ladder, chains rattling against the wooden bars. There were only half a dozen passengers and they were all comfortably settled under an awning in the prow where they caught what breezes were going. The rest of the prisoners already squatted in the stern and a couple of guards lounged on a hatch-cover, smoking and playing cards.

One of them glanced up as we approached. 'Over with him,' he said. 'And throw him well out. We don't want him getting into the paddle wheels.'

I took him by the ankles, Munro by the shoulders. We swung him between us in an arc out over the rail. There was a splash, ibis rose in a dark cloud, black against the sky, the beating of their wings filling the air.

Munro crossed himself. I said, 'You can still believe in God?'

He seemed surprised. 'But what has God to do with this, senhor? This is Man and Man only.'

'I've got a friend I'd like you to meet some

time,' I told him. 'I think you'd get on famously.'

He had one cigarette left, begged a light from the guard and we went to the rail to share it. He started to crouch. I said, 'No, let's stand. I've been down there long enough.'

He peered at my face in the half-darkness, leaning close. 'I think you are yourself again, my friend.'

'I think so, too.'

We stood there at the rail looking out across the river at the jungle, black against the evening sky as the sun set. It was extraordinarily beautiful and everything was still. No bird called and the only sound was the steady swish of the paddles. Munro left me for a while and went and crouched beside Ramis, the man who had already spent some time at Machados.

When he returned he said quietly, 'According to Ramis we'll be there in the morning. He says we leave the Negro about twenty miles from here. There's a river called the Seco which cuts into the heart of the swamp. Machados is on some kind of island about ten miles inside.'

It was as if the gate was already swinging shut and I was filled with a sudden dangerous excitement. 'Can you swim?'

'In these?' he said, raising his hands.

I stretched the chain between my wrists. There was about two and a half feet of it and the same between the ankles. 'Enough for some sort of dog paddle. I think I could keep afloat long enough to reach the bank.'

'You'd never make it, my friend,' he said. 'Look there by the stern.'

I peered over the rail. Alligators' eyes glow red at night. Down there, tiny pin-pricks gleamed balefully in the darkness as they followed the boat like gulls at sea, waiting for the leavings.

'I have as great a desire for freedom as you,' Munro said softly, 'but suicide is another matter.'

And suicide was the only word for it, he was right enough there. In any event, the moment had passed for the guards put their cards away, formed us into a line and put us back in the hold.

*   *   *

It was Ramis who saved me by cutting his throat just after dawn with a razor blade he had presumably secreted on his person, since Manaus. He took several minutes to die and it wasn't pleasant listening to him gurgle his life away there in the semi-darkness.

We were perhaps two or three miles into the Seco at the time and it had an explosive effect on the rest of the prisoners. One man cracked completely, screaming like a woman, trampling his way through the others in an attempt to reach the ladder.

Panic swept through the group then, men kicking and cursing at each other, struggling wildly. The hatch went back with a crash, there was a warning shot into the air and everyone froze. A guard came halfway down the ladder, a pistol in his hand. Ramis sprawled face-down and everyone stood back from the body. The guard dropped in and turned him over with a foot. He was a ghastly sight, his throat gaping, the razor still firmly grasped in his right hand.

'All right,' the guard said. 'Let's have him up.'

I moved before anyone else and got a hand

to the body and Munro, by a kind of telepathy, was with me. He took the razor from the clenched hand and I heaved Ramis over his shoulder.

There was blood everywhere. My hands were smeared with it and it splashed down on my head and face and I followed Munro up on deck.

The river was only thirty or forty yards wide and mangrove swamp stretched away on either side, mist curling up from the surface of the water in the cold morning air. Even then, at that fixed point in time, I was not certain of what I intended to do. Things happened, I think, because they happened and very much by chance.

A miserable village, half a dozen huts constructed on sticks above a mudbank, drifted by. There were a couple of fishing nets stretched out on poles to dry and three canoes drawn up out of the water.

It was enough. I glanced at Munro. He nodded. As the village disappeared into the curling mist, we moved past the guards with our bloody burden and went to the rail.

'Go on, over with him,' the sergeant in charge said. 'Then get this deck cleaned up.'

He was standing by the hatch smoking. Another guard sat beside him, a carbine across his knees. They were the only two on view although there had to be others around. I took Ramis by the ankles, Munro took his arms. We swung him once, then twice. The third time we simply threw him at the sergeant and the guard on the hatch. I didn't even wait to see what happened, but flung myself awkwardly over the rail.

I started to kick wildly the moment the water closed over my head, aware of the constriction of the chains, aware also of the danger from the paddle wheel at the stern. Kicking with my feet was easy enough and I simply clawed both hands forward in a frenzy, the turbulence all around me in the water as the boat slid past.

It would be some time before they could get it to stop, that would be one point in our favour, but they had already started firing. A bullet kicked water into the air a yard in front of me. I glanced over my shoulder, saw Munro some little way behind, the sergeant and three guards at the rail.

They all seemed to fire at once and Munro threw up his hands and disappeared. I took a deep breath and went under, clawing my way forward for all I was worth. When I surfaced I was into the first line of mangroves and in any case, the stern-wheeler had already faded into the mist.

I hung on to a root for a moment to get my breath, spitting out brackish, foul-tasting water. The general smell at that level was terrible and a snake glided by, reminding me unpleasantly of the hazards I was likely to meet if I stayed in the water too long. But anything was better than Machados.

I slid into the water again, struck out into the stream and allowed the current to take me along with it. I could already see the roofs of the huts above the trees for the mist at that point lay close to the surface of the water.

I grounded in the mud below the pilings a few moments later and floundered out of the water, tripping over my leg chains at one point and falling on my face. When I struggled up I found an old man staring at me from the platform of one of the huts, a wretched creature who wore only a tattered cotton shirt.

When I got hold of the nearest canoe and shoved it towards the water, he gave vent to some sort of cry. I suppose I was taking an essential part of his livelihood or some other poor wretch's. God knows what misery my action was leaving behind, but that was life. Somehow, in spite of the awkwardness of the chains I managed to get into the frail craft, picked up a paddle and pushed out into the current.

I didn't really think they would turn the stern-wheeler around and come down-river looking for me, but some sort of search would obviously be mounted as soon as possible. It would be when they discovered a canoe had been taken from the village that the fun would start.

It seemed essential that I got as much distance under me as possible. Whatever happened afterwards would have to be left to chance. Once into the Negro I would find plenty of riverside villages where people lived a primitive day-to-day life which didn't even recognise the existence of such trappings of civilisation as the police and the government. If I was lucky I'd find help and a little luck was something for which I was long overdue.

A couple of miles and I was obviously close to the confluence of the Negro. I was aware of the currents pulling, the surface turning over on itself. A mistake here and I was finished for I had no hope of keeping afloat for long in such conditions in my chained state.

I turned the canoe towards the left-hand side for I was at least fifty yards from the shore and it certainly looked as if I would be safer there. It seemed to be working and then, when I was a few yards from the mangrove trees, I seemed to slide down into a sudden turbulence.

It was like being seized in a giant hand, the canoe rocked from side to side, almost putting me over, I lost the paddle as I grabbed frantically at the sides to keep my balance and then we spun round twice and turned over.

My feet touched the bottom instantly, but the current was too strong for me to be able to stand. However, the canoe, bottom up, barged into me a moment later and I was able to fling my arms across the keel.

Things slowed down a little after that and we finally drifted into quiet water amongst the mangrove trees farther along and grounded against a mudbank.

I righted the canoe and took stock of the situation. The mouth of the river was about a quarter of a mile away and I didn't fancy my chances in the canoe, with or without a paddle. It seemed obvious that the best, indeed the only thing to do, was to attempt to cut through the mangroves on a diagonal course which would bring me out into the Negro down-river from the Seco.

I managed to get back into the canoe and pushed off, pulling myself along by the great roots of the trees until I came to a clump of bamboo where I managed to break myself off a length. From then on it wasn't too bad.

Henley, the Thames on a Sunday afternoon in summer. All I needed was a gramophone and a pretty girl. For a moment, I seemed to see Joanna Martin leaning back and laughing at me from under her parasol. But it was entirely the wrong kind of laughter. Some measure of the condition I was in by then, I suppose. I took a deep breath to brace myself up to what lay ahead and started to pole my way out of there.

13

Balsero

It took me four hours. Four hours of agony, tortured by mosquitoes and flies of every description, the iron bracelets rubbing my wrists raw so that each push on the pole became an effort of will.

The trouble was that every so often I ran into areas where the mangroves seemed to come closer together, branches crowding in overhead so that I couldn't see the sun which meant that I lost direction. And then there was the bamboo – gigantic walls of it that I could not possibly hope to penetrate. Each time, I had to probe for another way round or even retrace my route and try again from another direction.

When I finally saw daylight, so to speak, it was certainly more by accident than design. There was suddenly considerably fewer mangrove trees around although I suppose it must have been a gradual process. And then I heard the river.

I came out of the trees and edged into the Negro cautiously. It rolled along quietly enough and I had it to myself as far as I could see although as it was several hundred yards wide at that point, islands of various sizes scattered down the centre, it was impossible to be certain.

One thing I needed now above anything else. Rest, even sleep if possible. Some place where I could lie up for a while in safety for I could not continue in my present state.

It seemed to me then that one of those islands out there would be as good a place as any and I pushed out towards the centre of the river using the pole like a double-bladed paddle. It was slow work and I missed my first objective. By then there was hardly any strength left in me at all and each movement of my arms was physical agony.

It was the current which helped me at last, pushing me into ground on a strip of the purest whitest sand imaginable. No south sea island could have offered more. I fell out of the canoe and lay beside it in the shadows for a while, only moving in the end because I would obviously drown if I stayed there, so I got up off my knees and hauled that bloody boat clear of the water . . . then fell on my face again.

I don't know how long I lay there. It may have been an hour or just a few minutes. There seemed to be some sort of shouting going on near by, all part of the dream, or so it seemed. Perhaps I was still back in the Seco after jumping from the stern-wheeler? I opened my eyes and a child screamed.

There was all the terror in the whole world in that one cry. Enough to bring even me back to life. I got to my feet uncertainly and it started again and didn't stop.

There was a high spit of sand to my right, I scrambled to the top and found two children, a boy and a girl, huddled together in the shadows on the other side, an alligator nosing in towards them.

They could not retreat any farther for there was deep water behind them and the little girl, who was hardly more than a baby, was screaming helplessly. The boy advanced on the beast, howling at the top of his voice, which considering he looked about eight years of age was probably one of the bravest things I've seen in my life.

I started down the slope, forgetting my chains and fell headlong, rolling over twice and landing in about a foot of water which just about finished me off. I'm not really sure what happened then. Someone was yelling at the top of his voice, me, I suppose. The alligator shied away from the children and darted at me, jaws gaping.

I grabbed up the chain between my wrists and brought it down like a flail across that ugly snout again and again, shouting at the children in Portuguese, telling them to get out of it. I was aware of them scurrying by as I battered away and then the alligator slewed round and that great tail knocked my feet from under me.

I kicked at it frantically and then there was a shot and a ragged hole appeared in its snout. The sound it made was unbelievable and it pushed off into deep water leaving a cloud of blood behind.

I lay on my back in the water for a while, then rolled over and got to my knees. A man was standing on the shore, small, muscular, brown-skinned. He might have passed for an Indian except for his hair which was cut European style. He wore a denim shirt and cotton loincloth and the children hung to his legs sobbing bitterly.

The rifle which was pointing in my direction was an old British Army Lee-Enfield. I didn't know what he was going to do with it, didn't even care. I held out my manacled wrists and started to laugh. I remember that and also that I was still laughing when I passed out.

It was raining when I returned to life and the sky was the colour of brass, stars already out in the far distances. I was lying beside a flickering fire, there was the roof of a hut silhouetted against the sky beyond and yet I seemed to be moving and there was the gurgle of water beneath me.

I tried to sit up and saw that I was entirely naked except for my chains and my body was blotched here and there with great black swamp leeches.

A hand pushed me down again. 'Please to be still, senhor.'

My friend from the island crouched beside me puffing on a large cigar. When the end of it was really hot he touched it to one of the leeches which shrivelled at once, releasing its hold.

'You are all right, senhor?'

'Just get rid of them,' I said, my flesh crawling.

He lit another cigar and offered it to me politely then continued his task. Beyond him in the shadows the two children watched, faces solemn in the firelight.

'Are the children all right?' I asked.

'Thanks to you, senhor. With children one can never turn the back, you have noticed this? I had put into that island to repair my steering oar. I turn my head for an instant and they are gone.'

Steering oar? I frowned. 'Where am I?'

'You are on my raft, senhor. I am Bartolomeo da Costa, *balsero*.'

Balseros are the water gipsies of Brazil, drifting down the Amazon and Negro with their families on great balsa rafts up to a hundred feet long, the cheapest way of handling cargo on the river. Two thousand miles from the jungles of Peru down to Belem on occasion, taking a couple of months over the voyage.

It seemed as if that little bit of luck I had been seeking had finally come my way. The last leech gave up the ghost and as if at a signal, a quiet, dark-haired woman wearing an old pilot coat against the evening chill emerged from the hut and crouched beside me holding an enamel mug.

It was black coffee and scalding hot. I don't think I have ever tasted anything more delicious. She produced an old blanket which she spread across me then suddenly seized my free hand and kissed it, bursting into tears. Then she got up and rushed away.

'My wife, Nula, senhor,' Bartolomeo told me calmly. 'You must excuse her, but the children – you understand? She wishes to thank you, but does not have the words.'

I didn't know what to say. In any case, he motioned the children forward. 'My son Flaveo and my daughter Christina, senhor.'

The children bobbed their heads. I put a hand out to the boy, forgetting my chains and failed to reach him. 'How old are you?'

'Seven years, senhor,' he whispered.

I said to Bartolomeo, 'Did you know that before I intervened, this one rushed on the *jacare* to save his sister?'

It was the one and only time during our short acquaintance that I saw Bartolomeo show any emotion on that normally placid face of his. 'No, senhor.' He put a hand on his son's shoulder. 'He did not speak of this.'

'He is a brave boy.'

Bartolomeo capitulated completely, pulled the boy to him, kissed him soundly on both cheeks, kissed the girl and gave them both a push away from him. 'Off with you – go help your mama with the meal.' He got to his feet. 'And now, senhor, we will see to these chains of yours.'

He went into the hut and reappeared with a bundle under one arm which when unrolled, proved to be about as comprehensive a tool kit as I could have wished for.

'On a raft one must be prepared for all eventualities,' he informed me.

'Are you sure you should be doing this?'

'You escaped from Machados?' he said.

'I was on my way there. Jumped overboard when we were on the Seco. They shot the man who was with me.'

'A bad place. You are well out of it. How did they fasten these things?'

'Some sort of twist key.'

'Then it should be simple enough to get them open.'

It could have been worse, I suppose. The leg anklets took him almost an hour, but he seemed to have the knack after that and had my hands free in twenty minutes. My wrists were rubbed raw. He eased them with some sort of grease or other which certainly got results for they stopped hurting almost immediately, then he bandaged them with strips of cotton.

'My wife has washed your clothes,' he said. 'They are almost dry now except for the leather jacket and boots which will take longer, but first we eat. Talk can come later.'

It was a simple enough meal. Fish cooked on heated flat stones, cassava root bread, bananas. Nothing had tasted better. Never had my appetite been keener.

Afterwards I dressed and Nula brought more coffee then disappeared with the children. Bartolomeo offered me a cigar and I leaned back and took in the night.

It was very peaceful, whippoorwills wailed mournfully, tree frogs croaked, water rattled against the raft. 'Don't you need to guide it?' I asked him.

'Not on this section of the river. Here, the current takes us along a well-defined channel and life is easy. In other places, I am at the steering oar constantly.'

'Do you always travel by night?'

He shook his head. 'Usually we carry green bananas, but this time we are lucky. We have a cargo of wild rubber. There is a bonus in it for me if I can have it in Belem by a certain date. Nula and I take turn and turn about and watch during the night.'

I got to my feet and looked out into the pale darkness. 'You are a lucky man. This is a good life.'

He said, 'Senhor, I owe you more than sits comfortably on me. It is a burden. A debt to be repaid. We will be in Belem in a month. Stay with us. No one would look for you here if there should be a hue and cry.'

It was a tempting thought. Belem and possibly a berth on a British freighter. I could even try stowing away if the worst came to the worst.

But then there was Hannah and the fact that if I ran now, I would be running, in the most fundamental way of all, for the rest of my life. 'When do you reach Forte Franco?'

'If things go according to plan, around dawn on the day after tomorrow.'

317

'That's where I'll leave you. I want to get to Landro about fifty miles up the Rio das Mortes. Do you know it?'

'I've heard of the place. This is important to you?'

'Very.'

'Good.' He nodded. 'Plenty of boats coming up-river and I know everyone in the game. We will wait at Franco till I see you safely on your way. It is settled.'

I tried to protest, but he brushed it aside, went into the hut and reappeared with a bottle of what turned out to be the roughest brandy I've ever tasted in my life. It almost took the skin off my tongue. I fought for air, but the consequent effect was all that could be desired. All tiredness slipped away, I felt ten feet tall.

'Your business in Landro, senhor,' he said pouring more brandy into my mug. 'It is important?'

'I'm going to see a man.'

'To kill him?'

'In a way,' I said. 'I'm going to make him tell the truth for the first time in his life.'

* * *

I slept like a baby for fourteen hours and didn't raise my head till noon the following day. During the afternoon I helped Bartolomeo generally around the raft in spite of his protests. There was always work to be done. Ropes chafing or some of the great balsa logs working loose which was only to be expected on such a long voyage. I even took a turn on the steering oar although the river continued so placid that it was hardly necessary.

That night it rained and I sat in the hut and played cards with him in the light of a storm lantern. Surprisingly he was an excellent whist player – certainly a damned sight better than me. Eventually, he went out on watch and I wrapped myself in a blanket and lay in the corner smoking one of his cigars and thinking about what lay ahead.

The truth was that I was a fool. I was putting my head into a noose again with no guarantee of any other outcome than a swift return to Machados and this time, they'd see I got there.

But I had to face Hannah with this thing

– had to make him admit his treachery, no matter what the consequences. I flicked my cigar out into the rain, hitched my blanket over my shoulder and went to sleep.

We reached the mouth of the Mortes about four in the morning. Bartolomeo took the raft into the left bank and I helped him tie her securely to a couple of trees. Afterwards, he put a canoe in the water and departed down-river.

I breakfasted with Nula and the children then paced the raft restlessly, waiting for something to happen. I was too close, that was the thing, itching to be on my way and have it all over and done with.

Bartolomeo returned at seven, hailing us from the deck of an old steam barge, the canoe trailing behind on a line. The barge came alongside and Bartolomeo crossed over. The man who leaned from the deckhouse was thin and ill-looking with the haggard, bad-tempered face of one constantly in pain. His skin was as yellow as only jaundice can make it.

'All right, Bartolomeo,' he called. 'If we're going, let's go. I'm in a hurry. I've got cargo waiting up-river.'

'My second cousin,' Bartolomeo said. 'Inside, he has a heart of purest gold.'

'Hurry it up, you bastard,' his cousin shouted.

'If you want to speak to him, call him Silvio. He won't ask you questions if you don't ask him any and he'll put you down at Landro. He owes me a favour.'

We shook hands. 'My thanks,' I said.

'God be with you, my friend.'

I stepped over the rail to the steam barge and the two Indian deckhands cast off. As we pulled away, I moved to the stern and looked back towards the raft. Bartolomeo stood watching, an arm about his wife, the two children at his side.

He leaned down and spoke to them and they both started to wave vigorously. I waved back, feeling unaccountably cheered and then we moved into the mouth of the Mortes and they disappeared from view.

14

Up the River of Death

At two o'clock that afternoon the steam barge dropped me at Landro, pausing at the jetty only for as long as it took me to step over the rail. I waved as it moved away and got no reply which didn't particularly surprise me. During the entire trip, Silvio had not spoken to me once and the Indian deckhands had kept away from me. Whatever he was up to was no business of mine, but it was certainly illegal, I was sure of that.

A couple of locals were down on the beach beneath the jetty beside their canoes mending nets. They looked casually up as I walked by, then carried on with their task.

There was something missing – something

which didn't fit. I paused on the riverbank, frowning over it, then realised what it was. The mission launch was no longer tied up at the jetty. So they'd finally decided to get out? In a way, that surprised me.

An even bigger surprise waited when I crossed the airstrip. The Hayley stood in the open ready for off as I would have expected, but when I reached the hangar, I saw to my amazement that the Bristol stood inside. Now how could that be?

There was no one about. Even the military radio section had been cleared. In fact, there was something of an air of desolation to the place. I helped myself to a whisky from the bottle on the table then climbed up to the observer's cockpit of the Bristol and found the 10-gauge still in its special compartment and a couple of boxes of steel buckshot.

I loaded up as I crossed the airstrip. All very dramatic, I suppose, but the chips were down now with a vengeance and I was going to have the truth out of him for the whole world to see, nothing was more certain.

I tried the house first, approaching

cautiously from the rear and entering by the back door. I needn't have bothered. There was no one there. There was another mystery here also. My old room had been cleared of any sign that Joanna Martin had ever inhabited it, but Mannie had very obviously not moved back in for neither of the two beds was made up.

It was a different story in Hannah's old room. It stank like a urinal and from the look of things had very probably been used for that purpose. The bed had been recently slept in, sheets and blankets scattered to the floor and someone had vomited by the window.

I got out of there fast, my stomach heaving, and moved towards Landro, the shotgun in the crook of my left arm. Again, there was this quality of *déjà vu* to everything. As if I had taken this same walk many times before, which in a way, I had. The same hopeless faces on the veranda of the houses, the same dirty, verminous little children playing underneath.

Time was a circle, no beginning, no end and I would take this walk for all eternity.

A disquieting thought to say the least and then, when I was ten or fifteen yards away from the hotel, I heard the crash of glass breaking, a woman screamed and a chair came through one of the windows.

A moment later, the door was flying open and Mannie backed out slowly. Beyond him, Hannah stood inside the bar clutching a broken bottle by the neck.

It was Hannah who saw me first – saw a ghost walk before him. A look of stupefaction appeared on his face, his grip slackened, the bottle fell to the floor.

He was certainly a sight, no resemblance at all to the man I had met that first day beside the Vega. This was a human wreck. Bloodshot eyes, face swollen by drink, the linen suit indescribably filthy and soaked in liquor.

Mannie glanced over his shoulder. His eyes widened. 'God in Heaven, we have miracles now? You're supposed to be dead in some swamp on the Seco. We had a message on the radio from Manaus last night. What happened?'

'My luck turned, that's what happened.' I went up the steps to join him. 'How long has he been like this?'

'Fifteen or sixteen hours He's trying to kill himself, I think. His own judge and jury.'

'And why should he do that?'

'You know as well as I do, damn you.'

'Well, thanks for speaking up for me,' I said. 'You were a real friend in need.'

He said instantly, 'I didn't know till the night before last when he started raving. Didn't know for sure, anyway. Even then, what proof did I have? You were pretty mad when you left here, remember? Capable of most things.'

Hannah had simply stood there inside the door during this conversation staring stupidly at me as if not comprehending. And then some sort of light seemed to dawn.

'Well, I'll be damned,' he said. 'The boy wonder. And how was Devil's Island?'

I moved in close, the barrel of the 10-gauge coming up. Mannie cried out in alarm, a woman screamed, Figueiredo's wife standing with her husband behind the bar. Hannah laughed foolishly, took a swipe at me and almost lost his balance, would have done if he hadn't fallen against me, knocking the barrel of the shotgun to one side.

He had a stink on him like an open grave, a kind of general corruption that was more total in its effect than any mere physical decay. I was seeing a human being disintegrate before my eyes.

I lowered my gun and pushed him away gently. 'Why don't you sit down, Sam?'

He staggered back and flung his arms wide. 'Well, if that don't beat all? Would you listen to the boy wonder turning the other cheek.'

He blundered along the counter sending glasses flying. 'But I fixed you, wonder boy. I really fixed you good.'

Figueiredo glanced at me, frowning. I said, 'Nobody fixed me, Sam, I just got caught, that's all.'

The remark didn't seem to get through to him and in any event, was unnecessary for he condemned himself out of his own mouth with no prompting from me.

He reached across the counter, grabbing

Figueiredo by the front of his jacket. 'Heh, listen to this. This is good. Wonder boy, here, was running out on me, see? Leaving me in the lurch so I fixed him good. He thought he was taking his last mail run, but I slipped him a little extra something that sent him straight to Machados. Don't you find that funny?'

'Very funny, senhor,' Figueiredo said, gently disengaging himself.

Hannah slid along the bar, laughing helplessly, glasses cascading to the floor. When he reached the other end he simply fell on his face and lay still.

Figueiredo went round the end of the bar. He sighed heavily. 'A bad business this.' He turned and held out his hand to me. 'No one regrets what you have been through more than myself, Senhor Mallory, but by some miracle you are alive and that is all that matters. Naturally, I will make a full report to Manaus as soon as possible. I think you will find the authorities more than anxious to make amends.'

It didn't seem to matter much any more.

I dropped to one knee beside Hannah and felt his pulse which was still functioning.

'How is he?' Mannie demanded.

'Not good. He could probably do with a stomach wash. If it was me, I'd give him something to make him vomit then I'd lock him in the steam house and leave him there till he sobered up.'

'Which was exactly what we were trying to do when he attacked us,' Figueiredo said. 'You have come at an opportune moment, my friend.'

'How's that?'

He went behind the bar, found a bottle of his best whisky, *White Horse*, no less and poured me one. 'The day after your unfortunate arrest, Sister Maria Teresa came to see me with as hair-brained a scheme as I have ever known. It seems this Huna girl, Christina, who Senhorita Martin purchased from Avila, had persuaded the good Sister that if she was returned to her people she could obtain news of Senhorita Martin's sister and her friend, perhaps even arrange for their return.'

330

For a moment, I seemed to see again the Huna girl standing on the veranda of the house looking across at me, the flat, empty face, dark animal eyes giving nothing away.

'Good God, you surely didn't let her fall for that?'

'What could I do, senhor?' He spread his hands. 'I tried to argue with her, but I had no authority to prevent her leaving and she persuaded Avila and four of his men to go with her. For a consideration, naturally.'

'You mean they've actually gone to Santa Helena?' I said in astonishment.

'In the mission launch.'

I turned to Mannie. 'And Joanna?'

He nodded. 'She and Sam had one hell of a row that day. I don't know what it was all about, but I can guess. She told him she was going with Sister Maria Teresa. That she never wanted to see him again.'

Poor Sam. So in the end, he had lost all along the line?

'You've been in touch with them?' I said. 'They have a radio?'

'Oh, yes, I insisted they took the one the

military left in my care. It seems the girl went into the jungle the day they arrived and has not returned.'

'And that doesn't surprise me.'

'You think the whole thing could be some sort of trap to get them up there?' Mannie asked.

'On her part, perhaps, to put herself right with her people if she wants to return to them permanently. They'd catch on to the idea fast enough.' I turned back to Figueiredo. 'What's the latest development?'

'Huna have been seen near the mission for two days now. Some of Avila's men panicked and insisted on leaving. It seems Sister Maria Teresa stood firm.'

'So they cleared out, anyway?'

'Exactly. Avila was on the radio just before noon. Reception was bad and he soon faded, but he managed to tell me that three of his men had cleared out at dawn in the mission launch, leaving the rest of them stranded.'

'Anything else?'

'He said the drums had started.'

'Which was why you were trying to sober

up our friend?' I stirred Hannah with my foot. 'Have you been in touch with Alberto?'

'He's on leave, but I spoke to a young lieutenant at Forte Franco an hour ago who said he'd contact Army Headquarters for instructions. In any case, what can they hope to do? This is something to be handled now or not at all. Tomorrow is too late.'

'All right,' I said. 'I'll leave at once in the Hayley. Is she ready for off, Mannie?'

'Is now. She was having magneto trouble, but I've fixed that.'

'How come the Bristol's here?'

'Sam went down-river by boat and flew her back. Had to just to keep a plane in the air while I fixed the Hayley. Once that penalty clause comes into operation he has a fortnight to find another pilot. He still hoped something would turn up or at least I thought he did.'

He hurried out and Figueiredo said, 'With four to bring back you must go alone, which could be dangerous. Would a machine-gun help?'

'The best idea I've heard today.'

He beckoned and I went round the bar counter and followed him through the bead curtain into the back room. He sat down, grunting, beside an old cabin trunk, took a key from his watchchain and opened it. There were a dozen rifles, a couple of Thompson guns, a box of Mills bombs and quantities of ammunition.

'And where did you get this little lot?' I demanded.

'Colonel Alberto. In case of attack here. Take what you wish.'

I slung one of the Thompson guns over my shoulder and stuffed half a dozen fifty-round clips of ammunition and a couple of Mills bombs into a military-type canvas haversack. 'If this doesn't do it, nothing will.'

I returned to the bar and paused beside Hannah. He moaned a little and stirred. I turned to Figueiredo who had followed me through. 'I meant what I said. Lock him in the steam house and don't let him out till he's sober.'

'I will see to it, my friend. Go with God.'

I patted the butt of the Thompson gun.

'I prefer something you can rely on. Don't worry about me. I'll be back. Keep trying to raise Avila. Tell him I'm on my way.'

I smiled bravely, but inside, I felt considerably less sanguine about things as I went down the steps into the street.

I took the Hayley up and out of there fast. The last time I'd flown her to Santa Helena it had taken me forty minutes. Now, with the wind under my tail, I had every chance of doing it in half an hour.

When I was ten minutes away, I started trying to raise them on the radio without any kind of success. I kept on trying and then, when I was about three miles down-river from Santa Helena, I found the mission launch. I reduced speed, banked in a wide circle and went down low to take a look.

The launch was grounded on a mudbank, her deck tilted steeply to one side. The hull and wheelhouse were peppered with arrows and the man who hung over the stern rail had several in his back. There was no sign of the other two. I could only hope, for their sakes, that the Huna hadn't taken them alive.

So that was very much that. I carried on up-river, my speed right down, and passed low over the mission. There was no sign of life and I tried calling them over the radio again. A moment later and Avila's voice sounded in my ear with reasonable clarity although the strength was weak and there was lots of static.

'Senhor Hannah, thanks be to God you have come.'

'It's Mallory,' I said. 'How are things down there?'

'Senhorita Martin, the good Sister and I are in the church senhor. We are all that is left,' In spite of the distortion, the astonishment in his voice was plain. 'But you here, senhor. How can this be?'

'Never mind that now. I found the launch downstream. They didn't get very far, those friends of yours. I'm going to land now. Get ready to bring the women across.'

'An impossibility, senhor. There is no boat.'

I told him to stand by and turned over the jetty. He was right enough, so I crossed the river

336

and went in low over the airstrip. There was no sign of life there, but there was a canoe by the little wooden pier.

I circled the mission again and called up Avila. 'There's a canoe at the landing strip pier. Have the women ready to go and I'll come over for you. I'm going down now.'

I banked steeply and plunged in very fast, going in low over the trees. A final burst of power to level out and I was down. I taxied to the far end of the *campo*, turned the Hayley into the wind ready for a quick take-off and cut the engine.

I sat there for a couple of minutes waiting for something to happen. Nothing did, so I primed the two Mills bombs, shoved a clip into the Thompson, slipped the haversack over my shoulder, got out and started towards the river.

Except for the path which had been flattened by constant use as a landing strip, the grass over the rest of the *campo* was three or four feet high. Somewhere on the right, birds lifted in alarm. Enough to warn me in normal circumstances, but then it all happened so fast.

There were suddenly voices high and shrill, a strange crackling noise. When I turned, flames were sweeping across the *campo* from the edge of the jungle, the long, dry grass flaring like touch paper. Beyond, through the smoke, I caught sight of feathered head-dresses, but no arrows came my way. Presumably they thought me a moth to their flame.

It was certainly the end of the Hayley for as I turned to run, the flames were already flaring around the underbelly. I was halfway to the river when her tanks blew up, burning fuel and fuselage spraying out in a mushroom of flames. That really finished things off and within a few moments the entire *campo* was a kind of lake of fire.

But at least it put an impassable barrier between myself and the Huna, one flaw in their plan or so it seemed. I scrambled into the canoe at the jetty, pushed off and found half a dozen canoes packed with Huna coming down-river to meet me.

Even with the Thompson, there were too many to take on alone and in any case, I couldn't paddle and fire at the same time. There seemed to be only one thing to do which was to push like hell for the other side and that's exactly what I did.

A point in my favour was the numerous shoals and sandbanks in that part of the river. I got to the far side of a particularly large one, ibis rising in a great red cloud, putting what seemed like something of a barrier between us.

They were nothing if not resourceful. Two canoes simply grounded on the sandbank and their occupants jumped out and ran towards me, ankle-deep in water. The other turned and paddled back upstream to cut me off.

The men on the sandbank were too close for comfort by now so I dropped my paddle in the bottom of the canoe for a moment, pulled the pin on one of the Mills bombs and tossed it towards them.

It fell woefully short, but as on a previous occasion, the explosion had exactly the effect I was looking for. They came to a dead stop, shouting angrily so I gave them number two which turned them round and sent them running back the other way.

Even at that stage in the game I didn't want to kill any of them, but as I picked up my paddle again I saw that the others were rounding the tip of the sandbank a hundred yards north of me, effectively blocking the channel. Which only left the jungle on my left and I moved towards it as quickly as I could.

Undergrowth and branches spilled out over the bank in a kind of canopy. Inside the light was dim and I was completely hidden as far as anyone on the river was concerned. I paddled upstream for a little way, looking for a suitable landing place and came to a shelving bank of sand where a creek emptied into the river.

I turned the canoe in towards it, aware of the Huna voices drawing nearer, aware in the same moment of another canoe lying high on the mudbank inside the mouth of the creek, as if left there by floodwater, tilted to one side so that I could see it was not empty.

I splashed through the water towards it

and knelt down, groping amongst the broken bones, the tattered scraps of what had once been nuns' habits. They were both there, but I could only find one identity chain. *Sister Anne Josepha. L.S.O.P.* It was enough. One mystery was solved at least. I dropped the disc and chain into my pocket and started up the creek as the canoes moved in behind me.

I had about three hundred yards to go to the mission and it seemed sensible to get there as quickly as possible. I started to run, holding the Thompson at the high port, ready for action in case of trouble.

I kept as close to the riverbank as possible, mainly because the ground was clearer there and I could see what I was doing. I could hear their voices high and shrill, down on the river, and there was a crashing somewhere behind me in the brush. I turned and loosed off, raking the undergrowth, just to show them I meant business, then ran on, bursting out of the forest into the open a couple of minutes later.

The church was only thirty or forty yards away and I put down my head and ran like hell, yelling at the top of my voice. An arrow whispered past me and buried itself in the door, then another as I went up the steps.

I turned and fired as a reflex action towards the dark shadows at the edge of the trees, each topped by a bright splash of colour. I couldn't tell if I'd hit anything. In any case, at that moment, the door opened behind me, a hand grabbed me by the shoulder and pulled me inside so forcibly that I lost my balance.

When I sat up, I found Avila leaning against the door clutching a carbine. Sister Maria Teresa and Joanna Martin on either side of him. The American girl was holding a rifle.

She leaned it against the wall and dropped to her knees beside me. 'Are you all rights Neil?'

'Still in one piece as far as I can tell.'

'What happened out there? We heard a terrific explosion.'

'They set fire to the *campo* and the Hayley went up with it. I was lucky to get here.'

'Then we are finished, senhor,' Avila cut in. 'Is that what you are saying? That there is nothing to be done?'

'Oh, I don't know,' I said. 'You could always ask Sister Maria Teresa to pray.'

A drum started to beat monotonously in the distance.

15

The Last Show

There was still the radio, but according to
Avila, he had tried to raise Landro on several
occasions since he'd last had contact at noon
and I knew Figueiredo had been trying to get
through to him which meant something was
wrong with the damn thing.

I did what I could considering my limited
technical knowledge, unscrewed the top and
checked that no wires were loose and that
all valves fitted tightly which was very definitely my limit. I left Avila to keep trying and
went and sat with my back against the wall
beside Joanna Martin who was making coffee
on a spirit stove.

Sister Maria Teresa knelt at the altar in

prayer. 'Still at it, is she?' I said. 'Faith unshaken.'

Joanna gave me a cigarette and sat back, waiting for the water to boil. 'What happened, Neil?'

'To me?' I said. 'Oh, I jumped ship as the Navy say, before I got to where they were taking me.'

'Won't they be after you – the authorities, I mean?'

'Not any more. You see, strange to relate, I didn't do it. I was framed. Isn't that what Cagney's always saying in those gangster movies?'

She nodded slowly. 'I think I knew from the beginning. It never did make any kind of sense.'

'Thanks for the vote of confidence,' I said. 'You and Mannie both. I could have done with it a little earlier, mind you, but that's all water under the bridge.'

'And Sam?'

'Poured out the whole story in front of Figueiredo and his wife and Mannie in the hotel bar earlier this afternoon when

I confronted him. So drunk he didn't know what he was doing. He's finished, Joanna.'

She poured coffee into a mug and handed it to me. 'I think he was finished a long, long time ago, Neil.'

She sat there, sitting on her heels, looking genuinely sad, a different sort of person altogether from the woman I was accustomed to. Somehow it seemed the right moment to break it to her.

'I've got something for you.' I took the identity disc on its chain from my pocket and held it out to her.

The skin of her face tightened visibly before my eyes. She started to tremble. 'Anna?' she said hoarsely.

I nodded. 'I found what was left of her and her friend in a canoe on the riverbank. They must have been killed in the original attack after all and drifted down-river.'

'Thank God,' she whispered. 'Oh, thank God.'

She reached out for the disc and chain, got to her feet and fled to the other end of the church. Sister Maria Teresa turned to meet her and I saw Joanna hold out the identity disc to her.

At the same moment Avila called to me urgently. 'I'm getting something. Come quickly.'

He kept the headphones on and turned up the speaker for me. We all heard Figueiredo at once quite clearly in spite of some static.

'Santa Helena, are you receiving me?'

'Mallory here,' I said. 'Can you hear me?'

'I hear you clearly, Senhor Mallory. How are things?'

'As bad as they can be. The Huna were waiting for me when I landed and set fire to the plane. I'm in the church at the mission now, with Avila and the two women. We're completely stranded. No boats.'

'Mother of God.' I could almost see him crossing himself.

'We've only one hope,' I said. 'You'll have to raise some sort of volunteer force and come up-river in that launch of yours. We'll try to hang on till you get here.'

'But even if I managed to find men willing to accompany me, it would take us ten or twelve hours to get there.'

'I know. You'll just have to do the best you can.'

There was more from his end, but so drowned in static that I couldn't make any sense out of it and after a while I lost him altogether. When I turned I found that Joanna and Sister Maria Teresa had joined Avila. They all looked roughly the same, strained, anxious, afraid. Even Sister Maria Teresa had lost her customary expression of quiet joy.

'What happens now, Neil?' Joanna said. 'You'd better tell us the worst.'

'You heard most of it. I've asked Figueiredo to try and raise a few men and attempt to break through to us in the government launch. At least twelve hours if everything goes right for him. To be perfectly frank, my own feeling is we'd be lucky to see them before dawn tomorrow.'

Avila laughed harshly. 'A miracle if they even started, senhor. You think they are heroes in Landro, to come looking for a Huna arrow in the back?'

'You came, Senhor Avila,' Sister Maria Teresa said.

'For money, Sister,' he told her. 'Because you paid well and in the end what has it brought me? Only death.'

I stood by the window, peering out through the half-open shutter across the compound, past the hospital and the bungalows to the edge of the forest, dark in the evening light. The sun was a smear of orange beyond the trees and the drum throbbed monotonously.

Joanna Martin leaned against the wall beside me smoking a cigarette. In the distance, voices drifted on the evening air, mingling with the drumming, an eerie sound.

'Why are they singing?' she asked.

'To prepare themselves for death. It's what they call a courage chant. It means they'll have a go at us sooner or later, but there's a lot of ritual to be gone through beforehand.'

Sister Maria Teresa moved out of the shadows. 'Are you saying they welcome death, Mr Mallory?'

'The only way for a warrior to die, Sister. As I told you once before, death and life are all part of a greater whole for these people.'

Before she could reply, there was a sudden exclamation from Avila who was sitting at the radio. 'I think I've got Figueiredo again.'

He turned up the speaker and the static was tremendous. I crouched beside it, aware of the voice behind all that interference, trying to make some sense of it all. Quite suddenly it stopped, static and all and there was an uncanny quiet. Avila turned to me, removing the headphones slowly.

'Could you get any of that?' I said.

'Only a few words, senhor, and they made no sense at all.'

'What were they?'

'He said that Captain Hannah was on his way.'

'But that's impossiblé,' I said. 'You must have got it wrong.'

Outside, the drum stopped beating.

The church was a place of shadows now. There was a lantern by the radio and the candles at the other end which Sister Maria Teresa had lit.

It was completely dark outside, just the

faint line of the trees discernible against the night sky. There wasn't a sound out there. It was all quite still.

A jaguar coughed somewhere in the distance. Avila said, 'Was that for real, senhor?'

'I don't know. It could be some sort of signal.'

As long as we could keep them out we stood a chance. We were both well armed. There was a rifle for Joanna Martin and a couple of spares, laid out on a table next to the radio to hand for any emergency. But nothing stirred in all that silent world. The only sound was the faint crackle of the radio which Avila had left on with the speaker turned up to full power.

The light up at the altar was very dim now. The Holy Mother seemed to float out of the darkness bathed in a soft white light and Sister Maria Teresa's voice in prayer was a quiet murmur. It was all very peaceful.

Something rattled on the roof above my head. As I glanced up a Huna swung in through one of the upper windows, poised on the sill, the light glistening on his ochre-painted body, then jumped with a cry like a soul in torment, a *machete* ready in his right hand.

I gave him a full burst from the Thompson, driving him back against the wall. Joanna screamed, I was aware of Avila cursing savagely as he worked the lever of his old carbine, pumping bullet after bullet into another Huna who had dropped in on his side.

I moved to help him, Joanna screamed again and I turned, too late, to meet the new threat. The Thompson gun was knocked from my hand, I went down in a tangle of flying limbs, aware of the stink of that ochre-painted body, slippery with sweat, the *machete* raised to strike.

I got a hand to his wrist and planted an elbow solidly in the gaping mouth. God, but he was strong, muscles like iron as with most forest Indians. Stronger than I was. Suddenly his face was very close, the pressure too much for me. The end of things and the muzzle of a rifle jabbed against the side of his head, the top of his skull disintegrated, his body jumped to one side.

Joanna Martin backed away clutching her rifle, horror on her face. Beyond her, Sister Maria Teresa turned and a black wraith dropped from the shadows above her, landing in front of the altar. I grabbed for the Thompson, already too late and Avila shot him through the head.

He was gasping for breath, the sound of it hoarse in the silence as he feverishly reloaded his carbine. 'Maybe some more on the roof, eh, senhor?'

'I hope not,' I said. 'We can't take much of this. Cover me and I'll take a look.'

I rammed a fresh clip into the Thompson, opened the door and slipped outside. I ran some little distance away, turned and raked the roof with a long burst, ran to the other side and repeated the performance. There was no response – not even from the forest and I went back inside.

Sister Maria Teresa was on her knees again, prayers for the dead from what I could make out. Joanna had slumped down against the wall. I dropped to one knee beside her.

'You were pretty good in there. Thanks.'

She smiled wanly. 'I'd rather do it on Stage 6 at M.G.M. any day.'

There was a sudden crackling over the loudspeaker, a familiar voice sounded harsh and clear. 'This is Hannah calling Mallory! This is Hannah calling Mallory! Are you receiving me?'

I was at the mike in an instant and switched over. 'I hear you, Sam, loud and clear. Where are you?'

'About five minutes away down-river if my night navigation's anything like as brilliant as it used to be.'

'In the Bristol?'

'That's it, kid, just like old times.'

There was something different in his voice, something I'd never heard before. A kind of joy, if you like, although I know that sounds absurd.

'I'm going to try and land on that big sand-bank in the middle of the river. The one directly in front of the jetty, but I'm going to need some light on the situation.'

'What do you suggest?'

'Hell, I don't know. What about setting fire to the bloody place?'

I glanced at Avila. He nodded. I said, 'Okay, Sam, we're on our way.'

His voice crackled back sharply, 'Just one thing, kid. I can squeeze two in the observer's cockpit – no more. That means you and Avila lose out.'

'I came floating down-river once,' I said. 'I can do it again.'

But there was no hope of that. I knew it and so did Joanna Martin. She put a hand on my sleeve and I straightened. 'Neil, there must be a way. There's got to be.'

It was Avila who answered for me. 'If we don't go out now, senhor, there is no point in going at all.'

There was a can of paraffin for the lantern in the vestry. I spilled some on the floor and ran a trail out to the front door. Avila slung his carbine over his shoulder, turned down the storm lantern and held it under his jacket. I opened the door and he slipped out into the darkness, making for the bungalows.

I gave him a moment, then went out myself, the can of paraffin in one hand, the Thompson in the other, my target, the hospital and administrative building.

Somewhere quite close at hand as if from nowhere, there was the drone of the Bristol's engine. Time was running out. Of the Huna there was no sign. It was as if they had never existed. The door into the hospital was open. I unscrewed the cap of the can, splashed paraffin inside, then moved back out and flung the rest up over the roof.

On the other side of the compound, flames flowered in the night as one of the bungalows started to burn. I saw Avila quite clearly running to the next one, a burning brand in one hand, reaching up to touch the thatch.

I struck a match, dropped it into the entrance and jumped back hurriedly as a line of flames raced across the floor. With a sudden whoof and a kind of minor explosion, it broke through to the roof.

And then all hell broke loose. Those shrill Huna voices buzzed angrily over there in the forest like bees disturbed in the hive. They burst out in a ragged line, I loosed off a long burst, turned and ran towards the church as the arrows started to hum.

Avila was on a converging course. I heard him cry out, was aware, out of the corner of my eye, that he had stumbled. He kept on running for a while, then pitched on his face a few feet away from the church steps, an arrow in his back under the left shoulder blade.

I turned, dropping to one knee and emptied the magazine in a wide arc across the compound and yet there was nothing to see. Only the voices crying shrilly beyond the flames, the occasional arrow curving through the smoke.

Avila was hauling himself painfully up the steps, Joanna already had the door open. I took him by the collar and dragged him inside, kicking the door shut behind me. I rammed home the bolt and when I turned, Sister Maria Teresa was on her knees beside him, trying to examine the wound. He turned over, snapping the shaft. There was blood on his mouth. He pushed her away violently and reached a hand out to me.

I dropped to one knee beside him. He said, 'Maybe you can still make it, senhor. Torch the church and run for it. God won't mind.' His other hand groped in his jacket pocket, came out clutching a small linen bag. 'Have a drink on me, my friend. Good luck.'

And then he brought up more blood than I would have thought possible and lay still.

Hannah's voice boomed over the speaker. 'Beautiful, kid, just beautiful. What a show. Are you getting this?'

I reached for the mike. 'Loud and clear, Sam. Avila just bought it. I'm bringing the women out now.'

'Wait on the bank and don't cross till I'm down,' he said. 'I've got the other Thompson with me. I'll give you covering fire. Christ, I wish I'd a couple of Vickers on this thing. I'd give the bastards something to remember.' He laughed out loud. 'I'll be seeing you, kid.'

Sister Maria Teresa was on her knees beside Avila, lips moving in prayer. I dragged her up roughly. 'No time for that new. We'll leave by the vestry door. Once you're outside run

359

for the river and don't look back. And I'd
get that habit off if I were you, Sister, unless
you want to drown.'

She seemed dazed as if not understanding
what was happening, her mind, I think,
temporarily rejecting the terrible reality.
Joanna took charge then, literally tearing the
habit off her, turning her within seconds to
another person entirely. A small, frail woman
in a cotton shift with iron-grey hair close-
cropped to the head.

I hustled them into the vestry, opened the
door cautiously and peered out. The Bristol
was very close now, circling somewhere overhead. The river was perhaps sixty or seventy
yards away.

I pushed them out into the darkness,
struck a match, dropped it into the pool of
paraffin I had left earlier. Flames roared
across the floor into the church. I had a final
glimpse of the altar, the Holy Mother
standing above it, the Child in her arms, a
symbol of something surely, then I turned
and ran.

*   *   *

I slid down the bank to join Joanna and Sister Maria Teresa in the shallows below. Flames danced in the dark waters, smoke drifted across in a billowing cloud, a scene from hell.

I could not hear the Huna for there was only one sound then, the roaring of the engine as the Bristol came in low. And suddenly he was there, bursting out of the smoke a hundred feet above the river, the Black Baron coming in for his last show.

It needed a genius and there was one on hand that night. He judged the landing with absolute perfection, his wheels touched down at the very ultimate tip of the sandbank, giving himself the whole two-hundred-yard length to pull up in.

He rushed past, water spraying up from the wheels in two great waves and I saw him clearly, the black leather helmet, the goggles, white scarf streaming out behind him.

I shove the women out into the water, held the Thompson over my head and went after them. It wasn't particularly deep, four or five feet at the most, but the current was strong and it was taking them all their time to force a passage.

Hannah was already taxiing back to the other end of the sandbank. He turned into the wind, ready for take-off, and then the engine cut. Out of the night behind us, voices lifted high above the flames, the Huna in full cry.

Hannah was out of the Bristol now, standing at the edge of the sandbank; firing his Thompson gun across the channel. I didn't look back, I had other things on my mind. Sister Maria Teresa slipped sideways, caught by the current. I flung myself forward getting a hand to her just in time, another to Joanna. For a moment things hung in the balance, the current pushing against us and then we were ploughing through the shallows and up on to the sandbank.

There must have been a hundred Huna at least on the riverbank, outlined clearly against the flames. At that distance most of their arrows were falling short, but already some were sliding down into the water.

When the Thompson emptied, he slipped in another magazine and commenced firing again. I gave Joanna a leg up into the observer's cockpit, then shoved Sister Maria Teresa up after her.

Hannah backed up to join me. 'Better get in and get this thing started, kid.'

'What about you?'

'Can you turn that prop on your own?'

There was no argument there. I climbed up into the cockpit and made ready to go. He emptied the Thompson gun at the dark line now halfway across the channel, then dropped it to the sand and ran round to the front of the machine.

'Ready,' he yelled.

I nodded and wound the starting magneto. He heaved on the propeller. The engine roared into life. Hannah jumped to one side.

I leaned out of the cockpit. 'The wing,' I cried. 'Get on the wing.'

He waved, ducked under the lower port wing and flung himself across it, grasping the leading edge with his gloved hands. There was a chance, just a chance that it might work.

I thrust the throttle open and started down the sandbank as the first of the Huna came up out of the water. Fifty or sixty yards and I had the tail up, but that was going to be all for the drag from his body was too much to take. I knew it and so did he – he was too good a pilot not to.

One moment he was there, the next he had gone, releasing his grip on the leading edge, sliding back to the sand. The Bristol seemed to leap forward, I pulled the stick back and we lifted off.

I had time for one quick glance over my shoulder. He had got to his feet, was standing, feet apart facing them, firing his automatic coolly.

And then the dark wave rolled over him like the tide covering the shore.

16

Downriver

'The *comandante* will not keep you waiting long, senhor. Please to be seated. A cigarette, perhaps?'

The sergeant was very obviously putting himself out considerably on my behalf so I met him halfway and accepted the cigarette.

So, once again I found myself outside the *comandante's* office in Manaus and for one wild and uncertain moment, I wondered if it was then or now and whether anything had really happened.

A fly buzzed in the quiet, there were voices. The door opened and the *comandante* ushered Sister Maria Teresa out. She was conventionally attired again in a habit of tropical white, obtained as I understood it, from some local nuns of another Order.

Her smile faded slightly at the sight of me. The *comandante* shook hands formally. 'Entirely at your service, as always, Sister.'

She murmured something and went out. He turned to me beaming, the hand outstretched again. 'My dear Senhor Mallory, so sorry to have kept you waiting.'

'That's all right,' I said. 'My boat doesn't leave for an hour.'

He gave me a seat, offered me a cigar which I refused, then sat down himself behind the desk. 'I have your passport and travel permit ready for you. All is in order. I also have two letters, both a long time in arriving, I fear.' He pushed everything across to me in a little pile. 'I was not aware that you held a commission in your Royal Air Force.'

'Just in the Reserve,' I said. 'There's a difference.'

'Not for much longer, my friend, if the newspapers have it right.'

I put the passport and travel permit in my breast pocket and examined the letters, both of which had been originally posted to my old address in Lima. One was from my father and mother, I knew by the writing. The other was from the Air Ministry and referred to me as Pilot Officer N. G. Malory. They could wait, both of them.

The *comandante* said, 'So, you go home to England at last and Senhor Sterne also. I understand his visa has come through?'

'That's right.'

There was a slight pause and he was obviously somewhat embarrassed as if not quite knowing what to say next. So he did the obvious thing, jumped up and came round the desk.

'Well, I must not detain you.'

We moved to the door, he opened it and held out his hand. As I took it, his smile faded. It was as if he had decided it was necessary to make some comment and perhaps, for him, it was.

He said, 'In spite of everything, I am proud to have been his friend. He was a brave man. We must remember him as he was at the end, not by what went before.'

I didn't say a word. What could I say? I simply shook hands and his door closed behind me for the last time.

As I walked across the pillared entrance hall my name was called. I turned and found Sister Maria Teresa moving towards me.

'Oh, Mr Mallory,' she said. 'I was waiting for you. I just wanted the chance to say goodbye.'

She seemed quite her old self again. Crisp white linen, the cheeks rosy, the same look of calm eager joy about her as when we first met.

'That's kind of you.'

She said, 'In some ways I feel that we never really understood each other and for that, I'm sorry.'

'That's all right,' I said. 'It takes all sorts. I understand you're staying on here?'

'That's right. Others will be arriving from America to join me shortly.'

'To go back up-river?'

'That's right.'

'Why don't you leave them alone?' I said.

'Why doesn't everybody leave them alone? They don't need us – any of us – and they obviously don't need what we've got to offer.'

'I don't think you quite understand,' she said.

I was wasting my time, I realised that suddenly and completely. 'Then I'm glad I don't, Sister,' I told her.

I think in that final moment, I actually got through to her. There was something in the eyes that was different, something undefinable, but perhaps that was simply wishful thinking. She turned and walked out.

I watched her go down the steps to the line of horse-drawn cabs whose drivers dozed in the hot sun. Nothing had changed and yet everything was different.

I never saw her again.

Standing at the rail of the stern-wheeler in the evening light and half an hour out of Manaus, I remembered my letters. As I was reading the one from the Air Ministry, Mannie found me.

'Anything interesting?'

'I've been put on the active service list,'

I said. 'Should have reported two months ago. This thing's been chasing me since Peru.'

'So?' He nodded gravely. 'The news from Europe seems to get worse each day.'

'One thing's certain,' I said. 'They're going to need pilots back home. All they can get.'

'I suppose so. What happens in Belem? Will you apply to your consul for passage home?'

I shook my head, took the small linen bag Avila had given me in the church at Santa Helena and handed it to him. He opened it and poured a dozen fair-sized uncut diamonds into his palm.

'Avila's parting present. I know it's illegal, but we should get two or three thousand pounds for them in Belem with no trouble. I'll go halves with you and we'll go home in style.'

He replaced them carefully. 'Strange,' he said. 'To live as he did and in the end, to die so bravely.'

I thought he might take it further, attempt to touch on what had remained unspoken between us, but he obviously thought better of it.

'I've got a letter to write. I'll see you later.' He patted me on the arm awkwardly and slipped away.

I had not heard her approach and yet she was there behind me, like a presence sensed.

She said, 'I've just been talking to the captain. He tells me there's a boat due out of Belem for New York the day after we get in.'

'That's good,' I said. 'You'll be able to fly to California from there. Still make that test of yours at M.G.M. on time.'

The horizon was purple and gold, touched with fire. She said, 'I've just seen Mannie. He tells me you've had a letter drafting you into the R.A.F.'

'That's right.'

'Are you pleased?'

I shrugged. 'If there's going to be a war, and it looks pretty certain, then it's the place to be.'

'Can I write to you? Have you got an address?'

'If you like. I've been posted to a place

called Biggin Hill. A fighter squadron. And my mother would always pass letters on.'

'That's good.'

She stood there, waiting for me to make some sort of move and I didn't. Finally she said hesitantly, 'If you'd like to come down later, Neil. You know my cabin.'

I shook my head. 'I don't think there would be much point.'

He was between us still, always would be. She knew it and so did I. She started to walk away, hesitated and turned towards me.

'All right, I loved him a little, for whatever that's worth, and I'm not ashamed of it. In spite of everything, he was the most courageous man I've ever known – a hero – and that's how I'll always remember him.'

It sounded like a line from a bad play and he was worth more than that.

'He wasn't any hero, Joanna,' I said. 'He was a bastard, right from the beginning, only he was a brave bastard and probably the finest pilot I'm ever likely to meet. Let that be an end of it.'

She walked away, stiff and angry, but

somehow it didn't seem to matter any more. Hannah would have approved and that was the main thing.

I turned back to the rail beyond the trees, the sun slipped behind the final edge of things and night fell.

What's next?

Tell us the name of an author you love

Jack Higgins Go ▶

and we'll find your next great book.

book army

www.bookarmy.com